THE WOODS OF FANNIN COUNTY

ALSO BY JANISSE RAY

Ecology of a Cracker Childhood

Wild Card Quilt: Taking a Chance on Home

Between Two Rivers (edited, with Susan Cerulean & Laura Newton)

Pinhook: Finding Wholeness in a Fragmented Land

Moody Forest (edited)

Unspoiled (edited, with Susan Cerulean & A. James Wohlpart)

A House of Branches

Drifting into Darien: A Personal & Natural History of the Altamaha River

The Seed Underground: A Growing Revolution to Save Food

Red Lanterns

Wild Spectacle: Seeking Wonders in a World Beyond Humans

THE WOODS OF FANNIN COUNTY

Janisse Ray

Cover art by Raven Waters, www.ravenwatersart.com

Cover design by Eleonora A. Machado

Author photo by Christopher Ian Smith,

  www.CISmithphotography.com

Set in Garamond

Printed in the United States of America

First printing, September, 2022.

Library of Congress Cataloging-in-Publication Data

Ray, Janisse, 1962-

  The woods of Fannin County / Janisse Ray.

ISBN: 979-8-9863064-0-7

independently published

Janisse Ray

895 Catherine T. Sanders Road

Reidsville, GA 30453

www.janisseray.com

4

for skye

Why is hate so easy and love so difficult?

—Wendell Berry, *Jayber Crow*

PHOTO OF THE SHACK CIRCA 1970s.

PREFACE

This is a work of fiction. It is based on a true story that took place during the 1940s in Fannin County, northern Georgia, in the foothills of the Blue Ridge Mountains. My late father heard the story first, many years ago. He convinced me to listen to it and arranged for me to meet a Mr. Woods, who had told it to him.

One Sunday afternoon my parents drove me to the Woods home, in the countryside of southern Georgia, down a long, light-gray dirt road bordered by cotton fields. I remember the weather that day. An early-summer thunderstorm threatened, and clouds like large purple bruises tormented the sky.

Later, from an oak dining table, I could look out a bank of windows and see the sky darkening over Jimmy Woods' well-kept yard. Mexican petunias were blooming. Mr. Woods had invited his sister from Alabama, who also had lived the story as a child, and she was visiting for the weekend. I sat scribbling under violet, circling clouds while the two of them poured out their fascinating and terrifying memories.

During a span of ten years I interviewed five of the eight people who'd been involved as children, and since those interviews, two of them have died. I studied historical and genealogical records to verify anecdotal information, visited the area where their cabin once stood, and researched extensively the time and place in which this story occurs.

This work is intended for an adult audience. It contains situations inappropriate for small children.

I would like to note that the main character in this novel, Bobby, is an amalgamation of the grown children with whom I spoke. Although the story is told in Bobby's voice, in reality I never spoke with him, because he had died by the time we began this project. Additionally, in the book Bobby accompanies his siblings when they are rescued. In real life, however, Bobby was too old to be accepted to the children's home, and, unbelievably, he was forced to strike out on his own at fourteen. Exactly what happened to him between fourteen and adulthood we will never know.

In most instances names of characters have been changed to protect identities and here are used fictitiously. Similarities with other real people are accidental.

Otherwise, the story is as close to the truth as possible.

Janisse Ray

Chapter 1

A forsaken mother sets off with eight children on an inexplicable journey by mule and wagon, 1945.

The boy awakened at sunrise to his grandfather's voice, speaking in low tones to the boy's mother, in the kitchen. The boy listened from his pallet on a hard and unforgiving floor, smelling coffee, then he folded back a quilt and crept to the kitchen door. As if sensing him there, Ruby threw open the door.

Git everbody up, she said.

In that moment the boy somehow understood that this was a day he would remember, even for the rest of his life. He felt surrounding him, touching him from all sides, a terrific and blinding secret, one that he would spend his entire life trying to uncover and also to decipher. He felt its hand across his mouth, he felt the secret pressing up against his back.

An hour later from a wagon box the boy, whose name was Bobby, watched his grandfather's team of mules plod up the short main street of Morganton, Georgia. Beyond the town the blue and softly rolling hills of the southern Appalachians interrupted the horizon and made the earth into a body.

The fresh morning sun crested the courthouse, pouring yellow honey over the buildings they passed, until the town appeared regal and inviting. The mules were shod and their hooves drummed on the macadam, a promising sound in the early quiet. The leather of the mule traces gleamed. The harness straps slapped against the mule bellies, which the boy imagined to be soft and warm. Bobby knew that Pet, a bay jenny, always hitched on the gee side, and Pat, a chestnut john mule with hind socks, on the haw. The boy had heard that they put up a fuss if they were reversed, although he had never seen them in any condition but placid.

The wagon passed Grady's Grocery, then the post office, then Morganton Drugs, where a few Packards and Hudsons were parked. Folks were already about, and they lifted their heads idly, and not so idly, as people will do, to watch the wagon.

Bobby kept his eyes on the mules. Their tails swished against their own backs and against the wagon with a rasping noise. People would talk—*Mr. Allen and his gal, all them chillen, wonder where they going?* After his mama came back from Michigan with no husband and a passel of kids, including Bobby, people had tried to corner him. Was he Ruby's boy? Where was his father? Were they back for good? What had Michigan been like (pronouncing it *Mitchgan*)? He had avoided the questions, edging away.

He couldn't help but wonder why his grandfather this morning had come for them. Why in the wagon? Mr. Allen, as the boy called him, owned a car, a 1927 Model T, and Bobby had ridden in it twice, quiet in the jumpseat. But this morning the meager clothing of the children had been stuffed into burlap bags and thrown atop a couple croker sacks of corn. A few blankets and quilts were stacked and bound together with a length of twine, along with a thin, homemade mattress cover their mother had emptied that morning.

The boy hunched close enough to touch his grandfather's knee but he carefully did not. Mr. Allen wore a plaid work shirt and denim overalls. This was not the way he dressed when he left on the train, Bobby knew, because he had seen him heading to the station, wearing black pants and a black vest over a white, long-sleeved shirt, his black boots assiduously oiled. A gold watch chain had hung from his pants pocket. Even now Bobby could have glanced over and seen the fob dangling from the special little pocket that overalls carry. But he did not.

Bobby had heard it said that Mr. Allen was a tool and die maker, and that he made work trips even to Washington. Most of the year, however, he farmed. For some reason, when he was home, he went barefoot. He was barefoot now.

Behind Bobby the baby started to mewl. He heard a rustle. That would be his sister Phyllis attempting to comfort Jeannie, the baby. The jenny Pet lifted one long dark ear. The harness creaked.

Sit up straight, he heard his mother say.

Bobby crouched directly behind the bay jenny, watching the breech slide up and down as the huge muscles of the mules worked under their thickening coats. Heat from their bodies warmed the traces and released a hint of tallow, languid and even lugubrious in the cool morning, suggestive of hot biscuits with apple butter and other comforts that the boy could not dwell upon.

Old Mr. Hiram kept the mules brushed and clean for Mr. Allen, and the boy had seen him on an evening squatted in the open doorway of the barn, greasing harness. Hiram was slight in stature, weathered from fieldwork. One of his eyes looked east while the other looked west. The boy had never known Hiram to engage in any manner of unkindness, and instead had observed the old man's colossal patience with the mules as he tacked them up and down rows of corn. Some people are like that, he thought. It was a fact. Some people were not.

At that moment Bobby's eye caught a leather strap beginning to loosen. Mr. Hiram had missed something, he realized, a track of stitching beginning to fray. Bobby watched the strap awhile, until he decided he should say something.

Mr. Allen? he said, kind of quietly.

The man looked at Bobby, and on his face, stirred up like porridge, was a strange mixture of coldness and pity. Even in overalls the man held himself stiffly, proudly.

Shut up, boy, he said. *Ain't none of your bidness. You done asked.*

No, Mr. Allen. It's something else. Bobby wanted to point to the strap but was fearful, as if any movement at all would draw attention and therefore pain upon his head.

Allen said nothing and the boy was quiet. The strap was holding.

Close by on the street a bronzed and wrinkled farmer stared at them. Beside him a gaunt woman in a faded bonnet missed a step and caught herself.

Morning, sir, the man said to Mr. Allen.

Allen, straight-backed, nodded solemnly.

Morning, Ezra, Mrs. Brazell.

Mrs. Brazell kept nodding, as if she were counting, even after the wagon had gone on past. A boy about eleven hunkered at Allen's knee. In the back of the wagon a handsome woman with yet a figure and blond curls stared ahead, out beyond the town. One of the bigger girls was holding a baby.

Wonder where they going? the farmer said to his wife.

Hit don't look good, she said.

The wagon passed a barbershop and G.W. Harvey's Mercantile. At the fire station a tall black man was washing a Crossley Fire Truck, moving his rag in circles over the polished candy-red fenders. Like everybody else, he watched them come and he watched them go, and the boy knew then why his grandfather had come so early for them.

Beyond the firehouse a red-brick building served as the sheriff's office, and as the wagon approached, the sheriff himself came out on the wooden sidewalk. The boy knew him by sight. The sheriff was big-chested and able-bodied, wearing a bright blue uniform with a silver star, gun in holster.

Good morning, the sheriff called heartily. Mr. Allen clucked to the mules and drew up.

Howdy, Hawley, the man said.

Well, well, Hawley said, too cheerfully. *Looks like a nice day for a trip. How is everbody?* Although the sheriff spoke to the old man he looked at the woman.

Tolerable, said Mr. Allen.

I hear it's gone warm up quite nice today.

The pretty woman in the rig spoke. *We've got to git on,* she said almost petulantly. *Stand back, Hawley.*

The sheriff stepped back. *When you coming back down, Ruby?* he said.

The woman did not reply.

Let me know, he said.

The mules started up again and the wagon began to pass white-washed houses set close to the road behind white picket fences. In the yards pink and purple thrift bloomed. The boy especially liked the Washburn place, where Cherokee rose covered a side fence and the yard was animated with late-season marigolds and zinnias. At the Shuman house a bent man in dingy, ragged clothes raked leaves.

The wagon crossed a wooden bridge over a creek called Hemptown, although it looked more like a river than a creek. Through a scrim of trees the boy could see the largess of Lake Blue Ridge, formed from the Toccoa River, glinting in the golden and slow-lifting sun. Bobby could not remember a time the lake had not been there, although he knew that his mother remembered, and therefore his grandfather did.

The street turned to red dirt, the houses turned to shanties. Yard trees gave way to woods, mostly white pine mixed with shagbark hickory, sugar maple, and scarlet oak. Yellow fluttering leaves clung to low beeches, and the wagon went on.

The boy watched the trees, waiting for something to be revealed. Later he would remember how much of his youth he spent waiting—waiting for his mother, waiting for some providential gift to arrive, waiting for love. Even then he knew he did not want to spend his life waiting.

He watched the rumps of the mules, swaying back and forth. He watched the frayed stitching on the weak section of strap. Depending on how far they were going, it could hold. He waited. Then he dozed and when he woke the buggy was moving slowly across a valley. He could hear, above the mule hooves and the creaking wagon, the sound of a stream, and sometimes he could see its water moving across its stones. To the west one of the low mountains of the Blue Ridge rose, and a stony road turned off toward it. Soon the creek touched against the road and the old teamster pulled up his dray. He got down, limber and agile for his age, and disappeared into the woods.

You-uns need to relieve yourself, git down, said the woman, Ruby. *And be snappy about it unlessen you want to git left.*

Ruby herself withdrew toward a secluded overhang. The biggest girl, dark-headed and pretty, began to lift down some of the young children. Bobby came up close to her.

Glenda, where we going? he said.

I don't know.

I'd like to know.

Me too.

The creek was full of rounded stones and lined with moss. The children gazed toward it, silent as wraiths.

After a brief spell the buggy went on. It passed a few cabins and soon Bobby saw ahead an unpainted building with a low porch and a hand-lettered sign out front that said *Fiveash's*. A yellow-and-white feist dog jumped up and ran toward them, yapping. Bobby could tell this was a store, and he hoped that they would stop.

They did not. The old man sawed the reins sideways and turned the mules up a mountain road that ran beside the store. This wasn't a road, really. It was more of an overgrown lane advanced upon by sumac with its blood-red drupes, by poison oak, and by the flaming stalks of goldenrod crowding in from all sides. The road rose sharply, gullied and washed with stones.

Mr. Allen gruffly clucked to the mules and clipped them across their backs. *Git up*, the old man said.

Right away the wagon was lurching and pitching fit to break in two. After a few hundred feet of this the old man ordered the wagon empty. Bobby leapt out and from the back lifted down his little brother, Jimmy. The small boy was tow-headed as a straw broom and missing a front tooth. Bobby took Jimmy's hand and they began to follow the backboard.

I know now why Mr. Allen didn't bring his car, said Bobby.

Why? said Jimmy. He was almost four and still had his baby voice, whereas Bobby sounded grown.

It wouldn't take this. Not like the mules.

I'm hungry, Jimmy said.

I think we gone eat when we get there, Bobby told him, low.

Get where? Jimmy said.

Bobby shrugged. *Wherever we're going.*

Chapter 2

Bobby tells the story, 2010.

It took us years to realize what happened to us. We never discussed it, not for years. We were too little to talk about it while it was happening, and then later, at the children's home, we had a new life to navigate. Finally, sometime in the eighties, all of us got together on a Thanksgiving night, and we got to talking to one another. We were all grown and on our own by then. That was the first time any one of us ever said anything. We all knew—we remembered—although we'd kept it inside us all that time. We talked most of the night, trying to parse out what had happened.

It started with the word "remember." *Remember the cabin where they took us? Remember the wagon? Remember the hole in the floor? You remember that?*

That night we got to pour all our memories together, into one vessel. At first none of it made sense. So we kept talking. *What do you remember about Michigan? Do you remember living a while with Grandpa and Grandma? What did we live on up there? What about diapers? Milk for the baby?*

Now when we go back and look, we're pretty convinced that we were put there to die on a mountain in Fannin County, Georgia. That's about the only conclusion a person can reach. It doesn't register that a family, even a whole community, could do that to eight children they didn't want. But they did.

We talked about writing a book. We talked about it a lot. Strangely, however, we never did it. We never even got together much after that first time. When a child goes through something terrible, he or she has to deal with it in his or her own way, and sometimes dealing means moving away from the past as quickly as possible, as thoroughly as possible. But you can't run from it. It's always there, inside you, gnawing at you.

There are two reasons I'd want to write a book. One, I want people to know what happened. It's never been exposed. And two, I'd want people to know that, through it all, we survived.

I never could make myself get started. It brought back memories I didn't like to think about and still don't.

Chapter 3

The children arrive at a place in the hills they've never seen.

When Jimmy got tired, the boy picked him up. Jimmy was especially heavy because they were climbing.

The wagon lumbered upward along the old road, which had worn away in places where rainwater had run heedless across it. In its bed lodged boulders and stones, and tufts of grass grew in small pockets of bare grit. The road was flooded with maple leaves, recalling some recent storm. Above it the limbs of trees stretched, as if trying to close a gap in the canopy that the road had created or trying to comfort tree-neighbors on the other side. Sourwood flared gold.

The mules strained at their harness. They lost ground and for a minute the wagon looked as if it were slipping back. Bobby, carrying his burden, jumped from behind it. He tripped on a rounded rock and caught himself.

Whoa up, said the grandfather. *Son of a gun.*

The wagon stopped, its large box canted against a pitted slope.

There's a strap broke, the grandfather said. He stood up and glanced sharply backward for the merest second.

The boy lowered his head. He said nothing. He moved toward the weed-tangled road-edge and set down the child. *I got to rest a minute,* he said, real low, to no one in particular. He had managed to keep up with the wagon but his sister, carrying the baby, lagged behind.

Stay here, he said to Jimmy.

He started back down toward Phyllis, but his mother narrowed her eyes at him and spoke sharply.

Keep moving thataway, she said.

I think Phyl needs help, he said to her.

Ruby stepped toward Bobby and smacked him across the face. She didn't hit him as hard as she could have. The boy bowed his head and turned toward the shady spot where he had left Jimmy. His cheek stung. He could feel blood in his face, blood that had begun to rise the minute she turned her dark, calflike eyes upon him. His nose commenced to run, painfully, and he wiped it with his cotton sleeve.

The woman was walking again.

Bobby glanced back at Phyl, then he picked up Jimmy again and followed his mama. Out across the mountains, poplars turned yellow.

Richard, a middle boy, stayed to hand his grandfather a scrap of rawhide and an awl. He would wordlessly watch the old man cut a measure from the leather strop, shave off a foot-long lace, and tie it off.

Bobby could only haul Jimmy about fifty feet before he gave out. He switched the child from one hip to the other, then to his back, wrangling him like a sack of potatoes. The distance between them and the somber, ragged band led by his mother widened.

Bobby stopped and put down his little brother. The child's eyes were big in his head, his straw hair cut at home and needing another trim.

Where we going, Bobby? the child asked. Bobby stood with his back to the mountain. Across the old road ironweed bloomed purple pom-poms that formed cheering squads along the way.

You already asked that, Bobby said.

No, I didn't, said the child.

Hush, he said. *Don't let her hear you.*

In another quarter-hour the road opened to a flat apron of land traversed by a stream. He heard the woman say, *Here it is. Glory be.*

Sometime in the past a clearing had been logged and a house built, although the yard was now overgrown with ironweed, joe-pye, and bidens. A small house, unpainted, nestled against the mountainside, among galax, snakeroot, and mountain duff. Its door was closed. A chimney made of narrow, flattened stones rose above a wood-shake roof. Across the front of the cabin a porch stretched, high off the ground, overlooking the old road. The porch was held up by weathered two-by-eights and accessed by what had been a staircase of wooden planks set atop mossy stones. When the boy got close he could see that a number of porch-boards were missing, the ground visible right through.

A stream ran in front and to the side of the cabin, chortling down the mountain to join the creek at the road below. Head-high jewelweed thick with orange and yellow flowers grew along it.

His mother and two older sisters had reached the cabin and rested like crows on its steps.

Phyl arrived and laid the baby on her back on the porch, next to the woman. The baby, whose name was Norma Jean although they called her Jeannie, was fussing and starting to churn her arms wildly, like a tiny windmill.

Hand her to me, the woman said. The woman raised her shirt slightly and tucked the baby inside, one side of her red lips molded into a semicolon. The baby made small sucking sounds.

A bird sang off in the woods, a pretty sound like a flute Bobby had heard on the radio back in Michigan where there had been electricity. Bobby knew that Richard was listening, watching for the bird he was hearing. Richard was very interested in birds. Somebody had given him a book of birds about the size of a billfold, and he studied it all the time.

After a while they could hear the mules striking flint below. Behind them, the raw and dirty cabin loomed.

The woman, holding the baby, straightened and picked her way up the steps and across the porch. The door was strange, one door divided into two, a bottom section and a top section. The woman put her hand on a rusty doorknob at the top part and pushed it open. She looked around before she opened the bottom half and stepped inside.

The boy had a strange feeling in his chest, as if he'd found an entrance to a cave. He'd known this feeling the day they left Detroit.

We gone live here, Mama? Glenda said.

The woman dipped her chin slightly and looked off toward a window. Two of its four panes were gone, busted out, and beyond the window the trees breached. Through this aperture the tops of hemlock sheeted down into the valley, revealing an erratic display of yellow, gold, orange, and red sumac off to the west.

There's no other place, Ruby said, her voice distant as the blue hills.

The boy thought of his grandfather's fine, two-story house on Allen Street where they had lived until one night he awoke to the shrill and harrowing voice of his grandmother and what sounded like his mother crying. A few days later they had walked a few blocks to a loose and rickety gray house, where by night the children slept on an unswept plank floor and by day moved like timid atoms through the two rooms. That didn't last long and now they were here.

Ruby disappeared into a little room cut out of the main. She came back out. *It needs cleaning*, she said to herself. She had them unload the wagon, piling their belongings carefully on the porch. Then she told Glenda to get Phyl and bring buckets of water from the creek. Richard should untie a bag of corn and dip out a potful.

The rest of you go git me some wood, go!

A rusted iron washpot perched on three river stones at a firepit. Ruby trenched the ground under the kettle and began to lay sticks, crossing them at all angles, as if a heron constructed a nest by a marsh.

Go git me matches, she said to Bobby.

Yes'm.

I need a little of that hemlock straw yon, she said.

She arranged the straw, then struck a blue-tipped wooden match against a rock. She was determined, precise. She touched the match to the straw, which fizzed and sent up a thin tangle of white smoke before lighting blue and orange. Strands of hair had come loose from the woman's green scarf, and her face was pink, sweat beads lining her upper lip.

You sure are pretty, Richard said. Bobby felt embarrassed for him.

Ruby looked at Richard as if for the first time, her face absent of expression. She straightened and touched the backside of her hand to her forehead then her shoulder.

Richard smiled right at her and said it again, *You sure are pretty.* He went on. Bobby felt a sudden rush of pity. *One day I'm going to have a good job, and then I'm going to buy you a lot of dresses*, Richard said. *And enough lipstick you can wear it all the time. I'm about old enough.*

Ruby concentrated on the fire, feeding it. Then she poured water into the kettle and scrubbed at it before she wrestled it sideways and tipped out dirty water. *Hand me the corn*, she said. *And go get me one more.* She took the dipper of corn from Richard and sent him for another, then added creekwater to the iron washpot, then corn and more creekwater until it almost overflowed. The children stayed alert to her, as if she were a planet and they its moons, orbiting, saying as little as possible and doing whatever she asked of them.

By mid-afternoon they had explored the cabin. It was about twenty by twenty feet, one room walled off to the left of the front door. Ruby had sent them to gather ruffness, dried pasture grass, cut out of a meadow back down the hill a piece. The kids had gathered the grass by the armfuls, and Ruby had refilled the mattress, which looked to be two sheets handstitched together.

Except for their mattress, now pulled neatly against a wall, a wooden table with one chair, and a rickety pie safe, the cabin was bare of furniture. A pot-bellied stove dominated the center of the big room. There was a handbuilt fireplace on a side wall, full of wood-trash, flanked by two windows with missing panes. Everything was unpainted. The door was unpainted, and the kids played with it awhile, closing the top half and opening the bottom, then opening both halves, then closing the bottom only, until their mother told them to leave it alone.

All the kids followed Glenda silently to the creek, which they accessed via a vestigial trail still creasing the yard. Silver water flowed across a tiny dam and spun around in a small, clear pool.

Somebody built this, Glenda said.

A long time ago, said Richard. *Who lived here?*

I don't know, said Glenda.

Is this where we're gonna live?

I think so, said Glenda.

Do you like it?

No, she said. *Why would I like this?*

It has birds, Richard said.

Who cares about birds?

And flowers, said Jimmy.

I don't care about flowers either, she said.

Chapter 4

Bobby

It's a hate. I still carry it. I try to dampen it because all that's done now. That was years in the past. I'm old and they're dead. At least I guess they're all dead.

I tell myself, *We survived.* You know, one of my brothers got a degree from the University of Florida and became an architect. He was a tough-minded dude. One of them has a successful contracting business. Phyl retired from Publix. One has an antique store. We did better than survive.

So I try not to hate. It's hard, though. Hate rises in me when I think about it. Imagine, all these years later, something so bad and so scary that all your life you carry pure hate. You can't get rid of it. You can't set it down. There's no place to put it.

Part of it is the shame. Part is what we did, what I did. Looking back, I guess I shouldn't have done some of the things I did, even under the circumstances.

Chapter 5

The children puzzle out the first day.

The boy woke to the sound of muffled drumming. He couldn't tell where the sound was coming from. It didn't even seem like sound at all, but some kind of detonation, like little clouds of air exploding. He sat up on his elbows. Day had come although the sun was not yet hitting the valley, and the cabin was dim. The boy could see light on the sourwoods up the mountain, through a paneless window.

The baby was jammed next to him on one side in a wide wetness, and Jimmy was on the other, his head against Bobby's ribcage. All the kids slept on one mattress. The bed still smelled like dry grass but also like urine.

Richard's eyes were open. They were large and brown under his thicket of auburn hair. Bobby's younger brother was a quiet kind of person.

You hear that? Bobby whispered.

Thunder-chicken, Richard whispered.

What is it?

The drumming sounded again. *Ruffed grouse is the real name. I read in my book that they do that.*

It sounded like Indians, Bobby said.

He crawled headfirst off the straw tick and walked the cold pine to the door, skirting a huge hole in the floor. Through the hole he could see dirt under the house. *This place is about rotted down*, he thought.

Phyl was already at the blackening washpot, staring into it. The fire was dead.

Where's Mama? he said.

Still in her room.

Bobby gazed down into the kettle. Last evening his mother had looked through the children's clothing and picked out a single sock, ragged and gray. At the firepit she stooped and filled the sock with cold ashes, then tied off the top. Now the corn had swollen at least twice its size.

The lye makes it swell like that, he said. *From the ashes.*

I know, she said.

When Ruby emerged, her hair was tied up with strips of cloths so that she seemed more like a rag doll than a person. She wore her oldest dress. She did not offer morning greetings but told Phyl to start bringing water and Bobby to fetch wood. They watched as she drained the hominy, rinsed it with fresh water, then started the fire all over again. In an hour the hominy had boiled tender. It had fatback in it, which she fished out for their plates. When the baby cried she told the children to look away, unbuttoned her dress, and fed the child.

While they sat eating they heard a halloo from the direction of the unkempt trail. Mr. Allen appeared, carrying a croker sack. He was in overalls again, with a green and blue shirt and now brogans on his feet. He eased the sack down, and when he did, something clinked.

Just in time, Ruby said.

The old mules is slow.

Daddy, you et?

I done et. He touched a boot to the sack. *That's all I could git,* he said.

It'll do, said Ruby. *It'll be just fine.*

I reckon.

It'll only take me a minute, she said. She disappeared into the cabin and the children, vigilant, heard the axle of her doorknob shake in its gap. When she came out her hair had been combed and she wore a town dress. She looked at Mr. Allen.

I'm ready when you are, she said.

He turned wordlessly toward the trail.

Bobby, Ruby said, *I'm going to town to work. You-uns got hominy to eat. And your grandma sent you some things.*

Not their grandma, Mr. Allen said over his shoulder.

Your grandpa, then.

The last Bobby saw of them they were rounding a bend in the road below. The children could hear small stones disquieted or sent rolling by the feet of the short man in overalls and his wavy-haired grown daughter.

Jimmy got up and ran downhill. *Mama*, he called. *I want to come with you.*

The woman turned around. *Git back, Jimmy*, she said.

Jimmy sat down in the trail and started to cry. Glenda went to him and took his hand and lifted him up into the morning of the second day, the day of their arrival being the first.

That second day, after Ruby had gone, Glenda emerged as the natural leader. She was the oldest girl, curly-headed, sunny, and bossy. She pounced on the sack Mr. Allen brought and pulled from it a jar of purplish jelly, a cabbage, a mess of leather britches, and dried apples wrapped in a cloth. She took the things inside to their rickety pie safe, dusting out cobwebs and mouse pebbles before arranging the food. She found an old broom handle and tied some rhododendron twigs to it and set to sweeping.

Here, take out these bowls, she said to Phyl, handing her four pieces of chipped china. *We've got to get them washed.*

Phyl came back. *What about soap?*

Look for some.

There was no soap.

Well, just scrub 'em with moss, Glenda said. She was stacking the plates.

Bobby located boards in a lean-to behind the cabin, built to serve as a woodshed. There were a few sticks of firewood in there, he said. He reported another shed of some sort except the door was stuck.

Come on, Glenda said to all of them. *Get the baby, Phyl.*

Inside the shed they found two canning jars, an enamel pan with a hole in it, a ball of cobwebbed twine, the head of an axe, and a jug. The children hauled everything down to the small dammed area of the stream and rinsed the dust off. They left their things drying and began looking about.

Tracing upward they found a spring, flowing clear and cold right out of the ground, weaving its way down the mountain to the stream, then probably on down to the creek. The spring had no springhouse although someone had dug a shallow cistern.

We can drink this water, Glenda said. *And this is where we'll keep our milk.*

Milk? asked Bev. She couldn't speak in whole sentences. *Where milk?*

Not now, said Glenda. *When we have it.*

Where we gonna get milk? said Bobby.

From a cow.

Yeah, I'm seeing lots of cows around, said Bobby. *If that's what you call rocks and trees.*

Most people have a cow, Glenda said. *We will too.*

When do we eat? Beckie said.

Whenever, I guess.

I'm hungry, the girl said.

Let's go eat then, said her sister.

Anyone coming up the brier-thick trail, had there been anyone, would have been surprised to see a band of children, a perfect stairstep from baby to oldest had they lined up, eight in all. Bobby was the oldest, followed by Glenda, then Phyl, then Richard and Beckie. Jimmy and Bev were still toddlers, and Jeannie was the baby. They gathered around a warm kettle in front of an unpainted, dilapidated cabin, sitting around on rocks or squatted on bent legs, eating from a few old bowls and plates. Phyl had mashed up hominy and fed the infant, who sensed that something big was happening and did not fuss, although she needed and wanted milk.

Supper was the same as dinner except all of the salt pork had been sluiced from the kettle. Thus night fell, evening lingering as it lowered across the worried sky. *We're facing west,* the one named Richard said. *That way's the Pacific Ocean. Behind us, that way, is the Atlantic.* Bobby thought about the oceans, which were a long way off, miles and miles; he had never seen either of them, although he knew what they looked like from pictures in school in Michigan.

You know the spring? Richard was saying. *It runs out of the ground and into the stream. Then the stream runs down to Hemptown Creek, the one at the edge of town. You know where the creek goes?* Richard studied things like that.

To the river, said Bobby, worldlier than the others.

The Toccoa River, said Richard. *And the river runs to other rivers and they all join together and run all the way down Georgia until they find the ocean.*

The children sat drowsily.

It's hard to believe, Richard said, *that our water right here helps fill the Atlantic Ocean.*

Right at dusk a lonesome dove began to mourn, softly, *whoooo? whooo?* Off up the mountain to the north something cracked in the woods, like a twig breaking. The bigger children sat unmoving. That one crack was all they heard.

You know bears live here, Richard said.

Shut up, Richard, said Glenda.

He looked toward her, a wise expression on his little face. He wasn't being mean. *Painters too,* he said.

I said shut up, she said.

They had arrived on the first day. Ruby had left on the second. Now it was the third day. Bobby again was one of the first to rise, although he found Phyl already outside, standing by the fire.

Bobby stood on the unpainted porch and looked around. The mountains could be seen as beautiful the way they rolled off into the distance. Just below the house, beyond Phyl, the little stream chuckled without pause, rolling across its stones. He watched a wind stir the trees around the cabin and a puff of leaves let go. They twirled and twisted through the air. He could hear them hitting the lichened shake roof above him with scratching sounds.

He sat down on the edge of the porch and slid to the ground, avoiding a clump of hearts-a-busting blooming by what had been the doorstep. Phyl didn't look up. The boy went and crouched beside his sister. She was moving a large wooden paddle around in the pot.

You think she's coming back today?

No, the girl said.

Why do you say that?

The girl shrugged. She let the paddle fall to the edge of the cauldron. She sat down on a flat rock and hugged her knees with thin and freckled arms. The freckles across her cheeks were like brown flowers.

Why do you think Mama's not coming back today? he asked again.

The girl shrugged, twice now.

I think she's coming back, the boy said.

She's not coming.

But you don't know.

She didn't come back yesterday.

One night is different than two.

You like hominy? said the girl. She was poking at the ashes with a twig. She had a dreamy way about her.

It's pretty good, I guess, he said.

It's still hot, she said.

I can feel it from here.

Should we put some sticks on the ashes and get the fire going?

I guess so, he said.

I waited to ask you, she said. *To be sure.*

The boy said nothing.

I like it, she said. *I'm glad to have it.*

The boy looked at her.

The hominy, she said. She looked up suddenly, toward the cabin. *Was that Jeannie?*

I didn't hear anything.

Maybe a squirrel, she said.

Chapter 6

Bobby

Our father played for the Georgia Crackers. That's a team you don't hear much about anymore. It was a white team, and believe it or not, there was also a team called the Black Crackers.

Daddy was good at baseball. He played when he was a boy growing up in Atlanta, right on through school. Then he joined the Crackers. He was playing for them when he met my mother. The team had come to play in Morganton and Mama was at the game. That was a Saturday. The next day, I heard, he drove back up, and before long they were married.

Daddy quit baseball because of my grandma, whose name was America. I called her "Mrs. Allen," the same way I called my grandfather "Mr. Allen" just like everybody else.

They say my grandma was a Cherokee, but I don't know about that. She did have dark hair and darker skin than most people around there. She might have been a little shorter than other people—she wasn't much bigger than I was at the time.

If she was Cherokee, seems like a person who'd been persecuted would make all attempts never to persecute anyone else. Especially children who couldn't help their situation. They couldn't help it, not at all.

Once I overheard somebody say Mrs. Allen lost a couple of babies way back yonder, and maybe that explains why she was so mean. If I asked her for a biscuit, she would turn and walk away. Sometimes I think maybe all the meanness started with her, like she was afire and the flames crept along, the way fire will smolder along next to the ground and you don't even know it's spreading until you see smoke rising a few feet away.

But I think life would be a lot harder if you could see everything burning around you, burning down your life.

My grandma told Mama not to marry my Daddy. My grandma said she wouldn't have her baby daughter, a society girl and the prettiest of the bunch, married to a baseball man. That wasn't no life for a high-class girl like Ruby. Ruby deserved better.

Mama did it anyway, waited by the side of the road until Daddy came along in his black coupe, got in beside him, and was gone. That was Jan. 23, 1934, Ruby Allen married Roy Woods. I saw it written on a piece of paper. They went to the justice of the peace to get it done, and the man signed it, J.V. Beaver.

I was born in 1935.

But my grandma was right. Mama deserved better than what she got.

Things were good for a while, I guess. Daddy knew that baseball life wasn't no life for a married man. After Richard was born he went to the man who owned the Crackers. His name, I remember it, was Homer Nelson and he owned a bunch of car dealerships. Everybody was buying cars and he was real rich. I heard Daddy tell Mama about it when I was littler.

Speak up, the man said. *You're one of my workers?*

Yes, sir, Daddy said. *I play for the team.*

The Crackers?

Yes, sir.

What can I do for you?

Mr. Nelson, my wife's wanting me to stay home more, Daddy said.

Well, son, you have the choice, Mr. Nelson said. His voice was not curt or cruel.

I'd like to keep playing the home games, Daddy said.

That's not how it works, son, Mr. Nelson said. *I got a hundred boys like you, ready to step up and take your place, jobs hard to find these days. They'd kill for a job like this.*

That's when Daddy and Mama left Atlanta and came back to Fannin County, back to the big house on Allen Street in Morganton, surrounded by fields of bean and corn and those soft old blue mountains that scare me now, that gathered around us like stone-faced guards, holding tight to everything I needed and wanted, not letting anything go. They never felt comforting or protective to me. They felt cold and aloof, rocky and detached. Mountains remind me of Mama and her people, which should have been my people but they weren't.

Daddy didn't last in Morganton.

Chapter 7

The children reach out to the storekeeper.

On the fourth day the children spent many of their daylight hours ranging the woods. In a cove not far from the cabin they found a grove of pawpaws, although they called them hollyhocks. The hollyhocks hung pendant from small trees that already dropped yellowing leaves large as tobacco. The children sat on the duff and ate their fill, then they got up and walked on. They went slowly because of the little ones, handing around the baby.

They found a viaduct across the stream. It was no more than a pine beam four or five inches wide. The board stayed damp from water splashing below, and it was mossy and slick. They went carefully across, holding each other's hands, and on the other side, the trail was wild with brambles and thorns. They couldn't go far before stickerbushes turned them back.

Far above the cabin along the stream they found a stone fire-ring filled with matted brown leaves, some of the stones bearing stains of charcoal and soot, near some busted equipment—a barrel with a hole in the bottom the shape of an axe blade, a rotted chair, pieces of copper pipe. A small shelter had fallen and a few lengths of tin roof flaked into the forest floor.

It's a stillhouse, Bobby said.

Let's go home, Jimmy said. *And wait for Mama. Mama's coming back. I want Mama.*

Look at this, Jimmy, said Richard, and held up a small pot without a bottom.

No, Jimmy said.

You can have it.

And then Bobby said, *Nobody's coming back.*

Shut up, Bobby, said Glenda.

They returned to the cabin, ate more hominy, and waited.

Later that afternoon they explored in a different direction. As a band they straggled down the old trace. They got to the place where the mules had stopped, then the place where the harness popped. These two small memories gave them some relief. They kept going, fighting brambles and crushing fern, until ahead of them they could see Fiveash's Store.

The feist woke up and commenced to barking, then an old woman in an ankle-length skirt came out and stared at them. Her skirt was blue, overlain with a dingy petticoat the color of acorn meat; her white cotton blouse had washed to near gray.

The children were closer now and the woman had gathered her senses.

What do you-uns want? the woman called. Even a child can read volumes in the texture and tone of a voice. The woman's silvery hair wound in a bun.

Hello, ma'am, Glenda said. She brushed her hair back from her face. *We're just looking around.*

Well, best clum on back home, the woman said. *You-uns give me the all-overs.*

We thought to come in the store, Glenda said. Her dark curls hung down her thin back.

You got money?

Glenda was not easily deterred. *We won't hurt nothing, ma'am.*

I know you won't, the woman said. She turned discreetly and spat a clump of brown juice onto the swept yard. *Did you-uns' ma leave you-uns in the cobbled up dogpen?*

We're staying awhile in the house up there, Glenda said.

I knowed it, she said. *Tell yer ma I orter git the giverment on this.*

We were just wondering if there's a way to get back to town, Glenda said.

Walk, the woman said. *I reckon you'd all git there eventually, the painters didn't pounce.* She went inside and shut the door.

Glenda's face flushed bright red. She spun toward home and began climbing, a brooding, determined look on her face, as if she attempted to swallow something as green and bitter as a June persimmon. *Durnit,* she said after a while. *I wanted to see what was in that store.*

What good would it do? Bobby said.

That evening the kids held a forum.

Something's happened to Mama, Richard said to Glenda. *She should be back by now.*

Maybe she's sick, Jimmy said. *We need to go find her.*

Maybe she's having another baby, Phyl said.

She's not having a baby, Phyl, said Bobby. *She doesn't have a big belly and you have to get fat to have a baby.*

Phyl had Baby Jean face-down on her thighs. She was jiggling the infant and patting her back continuously. The baby made little noises and slobber threaded from her mouth to the leafy ground, where the kids were sitting around on rocks. The toddler Bev, her strawberry-blond hair wispy and tangled, sat beside Phyl.

No need to go find her, Phyl said. *They'd just bring us back.*

You-uns think they'd bring us back? Beckie asked, brown eyes round. *Way out here in the woods?*

Suddenly the trees turned silent and the forest seemed full of eyes, peeping from behind mountain laurel and rhododendron, white pine and poplar. The world was vast, layers of steep mountains just like the one they were on, one raising up behind the other, thousands of lonesome hollows filled with hungry eyes. Glenda glanced behind her. A chill descended, and when Glenda was chilled, all the children knew it and a chill prevailed upon all of them.

Only Phyl lived within her own bubble of warmth. She had learned long ago not to count on grown folks, or anyone for that matter, for comfort.

Chapter 8

Bobby

The place we lived was up in the mountains of north Georgia. People used the name Blue Ridge for the mountains and later, when I was old enough to study geography, I understood them to be the tail end of the Appalachians, a chain that stretched up the United States, all the way to Canada.

Fannin County sat next to the state line between Georgia and North Carolina. The interesting thing about the whole place is that it had belonged to the Cherokee. It was all part of the Cherokee Nation until 1838 when the Indians were rounded up and herded to Oklahoma in the Trail of Tears. They lost everything, and I mean everything. They lost their farms, their businesses, their fields, their smokehouses. Every damn thing got taken from them.

After that a part of Union and a part of Gilmer counties were put together for Fannin. Fannin County is mostly the valley between the Cohutta Mountains, which is a small chain of its own, and the main Blue Ridge.

Morganton became a town in 1854, and it was the county seat until 1895, when that switched to Blue Ridge, I'm not sure why. Blue Ridge sat about six miles from Morganton. Mineral Bluff and McCaysville were other towns in Fannin, and there were many even smaller communities, like Hemptown and Hot House and Sugar Creek. Where we lived up on that mountain was called Loving. I wish someone would explain that. It was a name that sure as hell didn't fit.

The Toccoa River was dammed in the 1930s so that Lake Blue Ridge came right up to the edge of Morganton. I guess someone wanted to make it into a resort town. That's where my mama was raised, and where her parents, who should have been my grandparents, lived. I'm sure there were plenty of people in Morganton who made plenty of money off the tourists, and I think my grandfather was one of those who did well, but gobs of people were poor too, very poor.

We were the poorest of them all.

Chapter 9

On the fifth day a snake crawls into their midst.

The next morning the children, chilled, decided to clean out the fireplace. It was full of brown leaves, matted on a pile of twigs that some itinerant had lain years before, who had departed before the fire could be lit. Richard retrieved a stout stick and began raking the firebrick clean. Suddenly one of the dark limbs writhed and he jumped back. *Whoa*, he said. A fat-bodied snake at least three feet long crawled out into the room. Glenda screamed the loudest scream they'd ever heard, a scream that hurt their ears. Jean started to cry, and then Bev and Jimmy, until all the little kids were wailing.

Richard seemed mesmerized. *Timber rattler*, he breathed.

Grab the baby, Bobby hollered, and *You kids get out. Get them out*, he hollered again. *Grab Bev.* He danced away from the snake, from one foot to the other. *I need the broom*, he called. He sounded as if he couldn't breathe. Glenda handed him the makeshift broom. He began to sweep the snake toward the hole in the floor. Every time he touched the snake with the faggot of rhododendron the timber rattler would coil up and lay still, head raised a hand's width above its body and tail wagging although it had no rattlers. The vibration against the floor was its warning. When that happened, Bobby would dance back.

Now Glenda had all the kids on the porch. They watched through the half-door. *You're gonna get bit,* Glenda said.

Bobby finally got the snake through the hole. It hit the ground below the house with a thud.

Check if there are more, Glenda said.

You think there's more?

I've heard of 'em bunching up like that. A family.

Bobby turned back to the hearth, wielding the broom like a poker and driving it into the debris.

They might have babies, he said. *Let's get all this mess gone.*

They don't stick with their babies like humans do, said Richard.

No way to be sure of that.

Burn them up, Glenda said. *The matches are behind you. Set it afire.*

Watchful, Bobby chose a match, struck it on a floorboard, and touched debris at the edge of the pile. It ignited and began to spread quickly. Glenda shrieked again.

Another one's crawling out, she said.

Bobby danced with a second and third snake until he had dispatched them through the hole. He had gathered a small handful of wood, and now the fire was healthy he tossed wood onto it. *We need more wood,* he said. *And we need to close this hole.*

With what? Glenda said.

I don't know. Lumber from the shack?

Keeping a close eye out for snakes, the older kids hauled the boards they'd found in the shed and arranged them across the floor.

Don't walk on these boards, Bobby said. *They may not hold.*

That evening after more hominy and after sunset, the children lay down together on the straw tick, feeling the comfort of the fire and watching it burn too quickly away.

Will the snakes climb back up? Jimmy said.

I don't think so, said Bobby. *Not with the boards there anyway.*

There's still a little hole.

It's okay, Jimmy.

How did it get in?

Be quiet, Jimmy. Maybe through the door.

Jimmy lay quiet. *The door was closed,* he said, matter-of-fact.

Snakes are scared of people, said Richard. *He won't come back with all us in here.*

He's been here all this time. How many days is that, Glenda?

Five, said Glenda.

Four nights, said Bobby.

Jimmy was quiet.

He was in the fireplace all that time, she said.

I guess so, said Bobby.

The children lay silent except for Phyl, who was sitting up in the bed, rocking Baby Jean. Outside on the mountain a barred owl called, answered by another, until the cabin seemed the center of a congress of owls, hooting and babbling.

Crazy fools, said Glenda.

Why don't we sleep in Mama's room? Jimmy said.

She'd kill us. This from Glenda.

Bobby got angry then. They could all feel it, through the flickering light of the weak fire and beyond into thick darkness resounding with a maniacal hooting. *This is a god-damned mess*, he said. *A shitcan of a god-damned mess.*

You can go to jail for cussing, Glenda said.

Shut up, he said.

Well, you can, she said.

Who cares? he said. But he hushed.

That night Bobby dreamed that the snakes came back, through the hole, the first one standing on the very tip of its tail until it reached its ugly, triangular head through the floor of the cabin, pulling itself up with the long, ropey muscle of its body, then turning back to help the others up. Bobby was trying to scream, to alert Glenda and Richard, and although he could get his mouth open he could not emit a sound. The scream was stuck in his throat like a rag in a pipe. He watched the snake crawl over to the baby and begin to eat her, starting with her tiny, perfect toes, forcing her down until only her small head stuck out of his mouth. She cried out then, and Bobby woke, too petrified to move, listening for a fat snake rasping across the straw of the tick, listening to the baby fussing, listening to Phyl reach over to pat Jeannie; and he felt humiliation, that he could not save them.

Chapter 10

Bobby

I remember one time Daddy took us to a baseball game, Glenda and me. It was spring and dogwood flowers looked like constellations of stars burning white against the dark trunks of Atlanta's trees.

When we got to the stadium, more cars than I had ever seen were parked in the grass lots and along the streets. Cars were everywhere, and around us people were getting out of them, ladies and gentlemen walking side by side through wooden gates painted red. The men took money out of their pockets to get through the gates. Inside were long steps that Daddy told us were bleachers and people were finding seats. The dresses of the ladies hung down over the steps. I'd never seen so many people.

Daddy told us to wait a minute and he disappeared inside. In a little while he was back, wearing his uniform. The pants and the shirt were white, striped with thin lines that went up and down. His shirt said the word CRACKERS in red across the front.

He bent down to the car window.

You-uns stay here, he said. He reached back in the car and picked up his cap. It was red with the word "Crackers" written in white loops across the front.

We want to come watch you play, Daddy, I said.

I have to work. Now he was putting on his tie. It was red too. *I can't be worrying about you. You stay right here, don't go nowhere.*

We'll stay where we're supposed to, I said. *If'n you let us come with you.*

Don't leave this car, he said. *You can keep the windows cranked down but stay in the car.*

Mama had got left at home that day. As he was leaving Daddy had tried to kiss her. *Don't be pecking on me,* she said. *All the girls will be hanging on you while I'm back at home, stuck with all this.* She looked around the kitchen. It had a gas stove and water coming through a spigot over a sink. On a wooden table in the center of the room dishes still lay from breakfast, evidence of grits and fried eggs crusting in streaks on mismatched plates. On the floor a rough pine cradle tipped as a tiny baby inside it moved in its sleep.

Nothing could dampen Daddy's mood. *Aw, baby, I wouldn't look at anybody but you,* he said. *And you know I'll be back quick as I can. You can listen in on the radio. Whatever's going on, I'll be thinking about you.*

She looked petulant, then gave me a quick, calculating look. *You're taking Bobby with you,* she said. *Glenda too.*

Sure thing, he said. *Come on, kids. If you need the outhouse you'd better go use it. Then get in the car.*

From the stoop I heard Daddy say, *Ruby, you know you're the only girl for me.*

For the first fifteen minutes of the game we sat in the car. We could hear people talking and laughing, and none of them paid any attention to us. Someone kept hollering "popcorn" over and over. All the cars around us made me giddy and I started naming every make and model I could see, Packard, Hudson, Ford.

Daddy had parked not fifty feet from the white fence, and although we couldn't see over it, we heard a gunshot go off on the field beyond and people began to cheer. The whole crowd started singing and then cheering again, and everybody sounded as if they were about to blow up with happiness. I could understand why people wanted to come, why Daddy didn't want to stop playing. Even if a person was hungry, all that happy noise filled up the spaces in a person's chest. A man started talking through a loudspeaker. Whistles were blowing and people were whooping and cheering and laughing, and every so often, a bat cracked against a ball. The sounds became intoxicating. We had heard baseball games on the radio but now it was like we were inside the radio, and yet the game was happening right in front of us, just over a tall paling fence.

I'm going to the fence, I said.

He said not to leave the car, said Glenda.

He don't know.

If he finds out he'll whip you.

You going to tell on me?

No.

I got out. I could see people but nobody was close and nobody was looking at me. At the fence I looked back at Glenda. She looked small in Daddy's Roadster. I motioned for her to come on, and she shook her head. The fence was taller than my head but in places the wood didn't fit perfectly together. A piece low down had busted out, and I could sit on the ground and through this peephole see a large section of the field, men in Cracker uniforms scattered around, and a line of men in blue knickers in a row behind home plate.

Before I knew it, Glenda was beside me and that's where we spent most of the game. We kept looking for Daddy but we never did see him.

Two things happened that day I never told anyone about. Actually it was three things, if I count sneaking out of the car as the first secret.

The second secret is that we didn't stay by the fence the entire game. When the band started playing and the ball players left the field for halftime, we scrambled back to the car. I saw a lot of things dropping from the bleachers while we sat there. After a while the game started back up.

Let's go see what's falling, I said to Glenda.

She responded by opening her car door, so I knew she was one hundred percent in favor of looking.

Mostly it was wrappers. Some were brown paper rolled into cones that had held popped corn. Some of the wrappers were stained with what looked like mustard and grease. I scoured the ground, moving toward the field, the bleachers getting lower and lower until I was hunched over. Near one wrapper lay almost half of a hot dog, the sausage nestled in its bun and slathered with mustard and ketchup. It had landed mustard side up. With my knees in the grass I reached for it. It looked pretty clean. I picked off a piece of grass and took a bite. Glenda came up beside me bent over, and I handed her the dog and she took a bite. Above us large boards shuffled with the weight of hundreds of people.

Something told me to look up.

A lady about forty was peering down. She wore a pink hat with pearls stitched into it and a tiny piece of white veil on top like a sail. Her eyes were blue as morning glories, with dark places in the center. Suddenly a loud cheer went up and she looked away.

Glenda passed the dog back to me and I took another bite. Only the end was left and I handed it off. I looked up again.

The lady's hand was hovering over the edge of the bench. She was wearing white gloves. She had something between her thumb and her pointer, a small silver disk. Without once looking down she dropped the disk. It landed exactly where the hot dog had been. It was a dime.

I picked it up and began creeping backward. As soon as I could stand I checked my pocket for holes and slipped the dime in my pocket.

Was that a dime? Glenda said.

I nodded.

Can I see it?

Later. You won't tell, will you? I said.

Never, she said.

When the game ended, we scooted back and tried to sit in the car acting as if nothing had happened. I was in front and Glenda was in the back. It looked like a million people surged out and walked past us, every one of them in a hurry. Glenda was the first finally to spot Daddy.

She popped over the seat. *There he is*, she pointed.

He was a long way off. How she'd seen him from that far I don't know. He was talking to somebody, a lady. The lady was in a dark-blue dress with large polka dots. Its skirt flared out around her legs. Daddy and the lady had stopped and were talking, face to face. He put his arms around her and she put hers around him. Then he kissed her.

He moved back as if saying goodbye, then leaned in and kissed her again.

Get down, I said. *Pretend like you're sleeping.*

That's how Daddy found us. I was curled on the seat, possuming, but my stomach was churning. He said he loved Mama but he'd kissed another lady. That was the final secret.

I never said a word about that.

I have a theory about secrets. They can save your life, but after a while they can kill you.

Chapter 11

The children begin to learn the lay of the land.

Five days passed before Ruby returned. The children knew it was
the sixth day because they were counting. They started with the day
in the wagon. That was the first. Their mama left the second day.
Four days later Ruby appeared.

Her hair was tied up in her green scarf and she wore what
appeared to be a pair of men's pants, brown. She carried in her hand
a small cloth bag. Glenda was in the front yard, hanging a handful of
Jeannie's wet clothes on a tree limb. She dropped what she was
doing and ran toward the woman coming up the trail.

Hey, Mama, she said simply.

Everbody okay? Ruby said.

We run out of hominy, Glenda said. *We was waiting on you.*

In actuality the kids had been without hominy a day. The day
before, stomachs tight, they had begun to roam for food. Now,
hearing Ruby's voice, the baby suddenly began to scream.

Bring her here, Ruby said to Phyl. Phyl had been mashing
hominy and feeding it to the infant. Soon Jeannie huffed desperately
beneath Ruby's shirt.

Glenda. Why didn't you make some hominy? I showed you how, Ruby
said.

I couldn't remember.

I ought to wear out your hiney for that.

I'll do it now. You're here if I have a question.

Now that she had stopped to nurse Jeannie and catch her breath, Ruby glanced around as if she found the entire scene distasteful, as if somewhere deep inside her a secret fire burned, a flame she could turn down in situations like this and turn up in others. Her lips were pale but she was not angry. Again, she looked as if she carried a suitcase packed inside her heart. She could leave even when she hadn't left. *Where's Bobby?* she said after a while. She stood, the baby over one shoulder.

Off yon, Glenda said.

Ruby stood taller. Her eyebrows twisted the barest mark. *Off yon where?*

He went to fetch some hollyhocks.

That exact moment Bobby appeared from out of the trees like a young revenant, carrying in his hands a clutch of large yellowish fruits. He saw his mother and quickened his pace.

Hey, Mama, he called.

Hey.

That was all they said but something in that small exchange charged the air with negative energy. In the house Beckie ran up and hugged her mother. Ruby picked up the next to littlest and examined her for a moment, then put her down. Phyl stayed back by the wall.

Git out of here, Ruby said. *I don't want to look at you.*

Without a word, Phyl high-tailed out the front door.

She looks just like Red, Ruby said. *That sorry, no-count bastard.*

The children stared at her.

Yes, your father, she said. *Sorry, no-count bastard. And she's just like him. Same hair and everything.*

Late afternoon they heard sounds from the trail and Mr. Allen walked toward them, followed by Mr. Hiram. Hiram, slight and bent more than usual, carried a wooden box that clinked as he walked. Mr. Allen bore a bulging croker sack across his back. A tad of hope bubbled up in the children, even in the littlest boy Jimmy, at the sight of the two men. They experienced in a transcendent moment the feeling of salvation, as if their own burdens had been lifted and dropped into Mr. Allen's sack and he was carrying it for them, would carry it away with him back down the mountain; and also some thought alighted like a bird on a post, that he might carry *them* back down with him. The children did not know what was happening, nor in that world *could* they know. The thing that would aid them most was the fact that children, more than adults, have an uncanny ability to live in the present. That would save them, if they were to be saved.

The two men set down their loads and briefly rested on the boards of the porch. Mr. Allen took a white handkerchief from a back pocket and wiped his face.

Daddy? Ruby said.

Mr. Allen stepped inside. The children heard Ruby's footsteps and she closed both doors. They could hear Ruby and Mr. Allen talking in low voices, murmurs like a small waterfall.

Hiram stood up and turned toward the porch. He studied it with one eye for a long time. His other eye looked off toward the woods. Bobby was watching him.

You-uns need some boards on this porch floor, Hiram said presently, face free of expression.

Yessir.

Hiram bent a little and focused on the loose gray dirt beneath the porch, perfectly visible through rotted planks.

I'd watch for vipers under there, he said.

Yessir.

He turned slowly like the workings of a clock, taking in the scene, young trees crowding up to the brokedown cabin, vale of ferns and jewelweed, the trickling stream down a ways. Then he walked slowly to the kettle. He had a limp and with every step he lurched to the right. Bobby followed him. Hiram's face was leathery and wrinkled and looked native as he leaned over and examined the contents of the washpot. Then he stood tall, took out a white handkerchief, and passed it across his face.

Mr. Hiram? Bobby said.

What is it, son? His voice was deep but with an unusual lilt, as if the tip of his tongue touched the roof of his mouth often. He was refolding his handkerchief.

We can't live at the Big House? Why, this house ain't nothing but a shack. You ought to see inside. They's a big hole in the floor. Plus winter's a'coming, I know that. A couple of days ago we cleaned out the fireplace. It was full of sticks and leaves, all kind of trash. You know what was in there, underneath the trash? Timber rattlers. Not just one but three. We lived in the same house with them things for four nights.

Heh, Hiram grunted. He had a railroad cap on his head and it twitched.

Why do they want to put us off up here? Bobby said.

God works in mysterious ways, Hiram said.

What does that mean?

Git along the best you can, I guess.

After the men left, Ruby made a fire on the pot-bellied stove and set about frying ham and boiling potatoes. She opened one of the bale-topped jars and ladled a pickled peach-half into each of their hands except she never gave one to Phyl.

The peach was a serious orange color, bright like the sun when it's going down and gets big near the horizon. Pitless, the peach made a little cup where the sweet pickling juice pooled and some of the juice ran down off the peach and collected in their palms. It smelled like vinegar and also like cinnamon and cloves.

This is good, Mama, said Richard. *Thank you.*

Trying to get a purchase on his slippery half while taking a bite, Jimmy's peach fell to the dirt. He stared at it and his face folded. Tears slid out of his eyes.

Bobby picked it up.

Never mind, Bobby said. *Let's go wash it.*

Give that un to Phyl, Ruby said. *Here, Jimmy. Take this un.*

You-uns all go wash up, Ruby said when the food was done. *Take these dishes down and rinch them.*

Sometime in the night Bobby woke to a hoot owl that seemed no more than a few feet away. Light streamed through the room and at first he was confused. Who had come with lights in the middle of the night? He turned his head. Outside the glassless window the moon, full as a liquor jug, had risen sufficiently to shine like a beacon, a bare bulb in a plank house, like a light on a train in a bog. The owl screamed again and he jumped. The old booger was in the chestnut tree outside the window. It could come inside the house if it wanted, and grab at him with its razor talons, pecking with its sharp beak into the soft part of his belly. He knew the owl was trying to tell him something. He wanted to jump up and kill it with his bare hands.

He remembered that his mother was in the house, in the bedroom, in her own bed. He drifted back to sleep.

Next morning early, Ruby had Glenda drain the corn, swelled four times its size, and use a bucket of water to rinse the corn once. She built up the fire again. *Git more wood*, she said, poking sticks under the kettle, and had Glenda fill the kettle with water above the line of grain. The kettle began to release small bubbles then to boil, and most of the morning it bubbled, twice requiring Ruby to call for more creekwater.

Mr. Allen had brought flour, and for breakfast Ruby mixed up hoecakes and cooked them in the spider. She poured daubs of sugared peach juice from the jar of the night before on them, and they ate the hoecakes out of hand. At the dinner hour she fried salt pork and boiled cabbage.

She hummed as she worked although the children did not feel a part of her good humor. They orbited, doing what they were asked, except for Bobby.

Once on a train he'd overheard a fancy woman say that you choose your parents but that didn't make sense. He didn't remember choosing his mother. Like he saw it, the grown folks got to choose most things, and looked like a mother would get to choose her children. Surely she chose him, Bobby, to come down from heaven or wherever babies came from and be her youngun.

Back when he was a little kid, back when they were up in Michigan with his Daddy, he thought that. He thought she wanted him. But now he knew that she didn't. Not just him, all of them. She wanted to be rid of them. Now she's down here and Daddy's up there, he thought, and they have a divorce, she doesn't want us. She wanted Hawley Howell the sheriff even though he had a wife already, and she wanted pretty hair—it *was* pretty, the way she curled it up on little strips of cloth and then brushed it out the next morning, shining and bouncing in the light, especially when she shook her head and laughed. And she liked to laugh. But not with us, he thought, which is how I know she doesn't want us.

He felt sorry for the other kids, because they couldn't remember when things were different. Mostly he felt angry. Almost overnight resentment had seeded in him and in order to control it he had to give it shape, and he couldn't do that at the shack with her humming to herself but acting hateful toward her own children.

He walked down to the stream past the viaduct and crossed over. What had been an old footpath was sealed with mountain laurel and rhododendron and all manner of briar and weeds growing in the path. He picked his way onward, bruising joe-pye with his brogans and breaking fir and hemlock out of his way. A few hundred feet away was an old barn, half fallen. It had been made of logs and once had been circled with a hip roof, all around, which was mostly collapsed against the building's ribs.

He went on. The briars ripped his legs through his britches but he stomped them down, slowly clearing a passage. The trail traversed a slope.

After a time he could see open sky ahead, and beyond that, what appeared to be a pasture. He came out of the woods cautiously, standing in the shadows for a few minutes to study the landscape. It was a large pasture, studded with gray rocks and knee high with grasses and little flowers, yellow and purple, like flowers are in the fall. Across the pasture he could see another barn, this one larger and painted dark red.

He felt as if he'd seen that barn before. He knew he had. He peered across the sun-bright pasture, which was blinding on his forest eyes. Far across he could see the outline of a few unpainted outbuildings, five or six cows, split-rail fencing. Suddenly he knew where he was. That was his uncle's place. He'd been there a few times, although, just as it was at the Big House in town, had only arrived as a tagalong and not as a guest and left feeling some unnamable thing he would later come to recognize as shame. Then he had arrived the front way, along Loving Road to where the highway banked sharply to the left and started up toward the ridge, then down a wagon trail to Uncle Grover and Aunt Meryl's place, a small clapboard house that Grover had built. Now Bobby was coming up from the back of the mountain, down-creek.

The boy knew not to approach directly. He began to circumnavigate the pasture, skirting the tree line, listening and deliberating. Had anyone been studying the livestock they would have seen red cows lift their faces toward him and begin to rotate their bodies, so that they could graze while watching a small dark figure making its way toward them. Finally the boy was close enough that he could hear then see someone working a mule in a field beyond the cows. He merged into the shade of the forest and crept closer, until he was directly behind the house.

Chapter 12

Bobby

One time I heard my grandma recite some poetry. She was sitting on the front porch with some of her kinpeople, my uncles and aunts and cousins. My mother was sitting there too. I sneaked along the side of the house and crept under it. I could hear the rockers creaking and everything they were saying. There was a good deal of laughing.

Mama, say your poem, somebody said.

Which un? Her rocker creaked.

The one about our people.

This un? she said. First she paused, and I could almost see her spit discreetly into a tin can, wipe snuff from her pale lips, and begin to recite.

> *Your people*
> *love my people*
> *like my people*
> *love your people.*
> *There never was people*
> *love people*
> *like my people*
> *love your people.*

Maybe there was more to it, but that's what I remember. *There never was people love people like my people love your people.*

I think it was a little poem children learn in school, something people recited when they gathered up entertaining each other on somebody's front porch back in the days before television and computers. I couldn't figure out whose people were loving my people. I didn't know whose people I was part of, if any.

I guess Daddy felt the same thing because he had wanted to go to Michigan to work in the lines. Mama went with him. They wound up in Trenton. I was little and I don't remember much but one time he fixed up a bicycle for me.

I thought about him a lot. I was proud that he was a baseball player. I knew he thought about us every day. If he knew where we were, he'd come get us.

I shouldn't have been so sure about that.

Chapter 13

Bobby wakes considering from all angles their predicament.

Some mornings when the boy woke he could not remember where he was but the chemical smell of wood ash or the cloistered mold of the forest floor would come to him, and he would lie on the mattress of straw with the collective weight of his sisters and brothers almost crushing him.

Although she'd been gone nearly a week the first time, after that Ruby came home every three or four days. When three days passed, the children would begin to say *She'll be home.* As time passed Ruby's sojourns away began to lengthen. Bobby had no idea how long her absences would grow.

Their fate bore so heavily on him he thought sometimes he wouldn't be able to breathe. He would lie feeling the load on him heavy as an ox, and he would panic because even as he dragged air into his lungs it fled from him. He would throw off a little brother that pinned his arm or the baby from against his thigh, and he would crawl off the tick and move to the door of the cabin, hanging his head into a new day.

The day he'd crept behind his Uncle Grover and Aunt Meryl's house he had stood a long time watching. A washpot was steaming over a small fire, and his aunt, in a checkered dress the color of ripe persimmons, came out and poked at it for a few minutes with a stick. Then she went back inside. Chickens pecked around in the yard and a rooster kept crowing, even in the middle of the afternoon. After a while Bobby had turned around and headed home.

With all the air in the world, why did it seem he could hardly get any? If his lungs closed down against a whole sky filled with air, he'd keel over dead. Then who would make sure the kids were okay? He tried to see into the future but the thread of time wound out for him.

Truth be told, he couldn't imagine what would happen. He guessed he'd lie dead until his mother came home, and who knew when that would be? The other kids would have to haul him outside, to the margin of woods, and make him a cold bed in the leaves, a stone for a pillow. He'd have to lie there all day in the sun and rain and all night in the mournful darkness, when all the mountain animals would, wandering by, come upon him. Skunks would come right up and pad all around him, sniffing. Bobcat, bear, raccoon, painter: any and everything would be drawn to him, and he would be no more to them than a rotten pumpkin or an old log crawling with worms. They'd likely start to eat him.

He didn't want this for himself or for any of the children, for them to turn to granite and then for the granite to fall apart and stink, or for their flesh to be torn from limb. The boy couldn't stand the thought of it.

Now he was gagging for air, his fingers digging into the splintering wood of the porch floor, or what was left of it. He was on his knees gasping for even a teaspoon of oxygen.

In Michigan he had befriended a boy in his class. The boy, Will, had a smooth face, wavy brown hair that a barber kept cropped short, and lively green eyes. He brought a bag of marbles to school, and at recess a few of the fellows drew a circle in the ground and played a game they called Banana Boat. The object was to use a log roller and shoot the others' marbles out of the ring without going out yourself. Outside the ring was the wide blue sea.

Will had invited Bobby home after school. Will lived in a house that had square columns on brick bases holding up the porch. There was a black iron fence with no gate and between the fence and the house grew flowers and shrubs. Bobby remembered roses, little white ones in bunches, and large yellow ones, and perfect pink ones. He wanted a rose garden like that. One day he'd have a rose garden. Will's mother came to the door as if she'd been watching for them. Bobby couldn't stop looking at her. She was one of the most beautiful women he'd ever seen, slim and curly-headed and smiling. His own mother was beautiful—he watched the way men turned to look at her—but Will's mother was different. When she shook his hand she looked right into his eyes, and hers sparkled like blue-green pools.

Did you tell your mother you were coming? she asked.

Yes, ma'am, he said, although he had not. His mother would be sewing a new dress for herself or shut in her bedroom looking at movie magazines. She might be gone into town. Wherever she was, she would not be worrying about him. Bobby felt guilty about lying to Will's mother but it couldn't be helped.

Will's mother had rugs and nice chairs and a large dining room where Will and Bobby drank a glass of milk, helping themselves to oatmeal raisin cookies from a plate in front of them.

Where are you from, Bobby? the woman asked. *Will told me you haven't lived here long.*

Georgia, he said. Bashfully.

Oh, goodness, she said, delighted. *So am I. What part?*

He told her.

That's in the mountains?

He nodded.

I was born in Macon, she said, *right in the center of the state.*

Yes'm, he said.

Have you heard of it?

No'm. Through the open window he smelled a sweetness that made him light-headed.

Because of Will's mother and because of his own mother, forever after that Bobby understood that Georgia women were more beautiful than other women. He decided that when he got grown and was looking for a wife, he would look only in Georgia.

Will owned a set of cowboy pistols and a cowboy hat, he had his own baseball mitt, he had a bicycle, he had a line of little metal cars. When the time came to leave, Will's mother put a thin and lavender-smelling arm around Bobby's shoulders and slipped a paper sack into his hand.

Nice to meet you, she said. *Come back. And tell your mother I'd like to meet her. We Georgia girls would have a lot to talk about.* She laughed lightly.

Now, choking, Bobby thought of that moment. The rubber band that had his lungs squeezed in a wad loosened, and he started to breathe again. He could smell the cinnamon of the oatmeal raisin cookies he'd found in the sack, the lavender talcum, the intoxicating and ethereal perfume of the roses.

Bobby lived only seven or eight blocks from Will, yet Bobby's neighborhood was a greasier, dirtier, louder place. Although it was his home, he had not been able to find a place for himself. Too many children ran about, chasing and yelling at each other. Pebbles and acorns flew through the air. Fly swatters and rolled-up magazines kept coming at him. A silver maple in his backyard offered some peace for a while, until it didn't.

Bobby rose, breathing now, and climbed off the porch. He was shivering. He headed barefoot up the mountain, his stomach hardened inside him. He had found a boulder that jutted out from the hill, among a ring of laurel, and now he went there. Some kind of yellow bird flew from the laurel, followed by a small black bird with an orange stripe down its wing. Bobby climbed the cold damp rock and hugged his knees to his bony chest. His mother had come on Saturday. She had refilled the washpot with corn and boiled another making of hominy. She had brought a jar of pear preserves and had given each of them a spoonful with their cornbread. Everybody except Phyl.

On Sunday she left. Thinking of her, how her mouth was restricted and her eyes were hard, how she did not touch them, how she softened for the baby but not permanently, destroyed something inside the boy. He put his forehead against his knees and in the cool green shadows of the mountain he sobbed as only a boy can sob, shamefully, painfully, privately, and angrily.

Chapter 14

Bobby

I have tried to get a handle on the hate. I don't say I hate my mother. I say that I have no love in my heart for her.

There's a difference.

I wish I had love for her but I don't.

But if there's any defense for some of the things she did, you've got to remember that as a young woman she was supposed to be the brightest star in town. Then she had ten children in ten years. Apparently two of them were stillborn. She was not even twenty years old when the first one was born.

I have no malice in my heart because of that. If there's any cause for forgiveness, that's it. There were times that she did the best she could do. The malice I have in my heart is the way she treated us, Phyl especially.

Chapter 15

Without fire and matches, the children try again at the store.

Ruby was gone again. One day the hominy was finished and Glenda, as the oldest girl, worried. Before the hominy had run out she had scoured the kitchen and come up with a small cloth sack of flour. At dinner the children sat around the table and ate spoonfuls raw.

I could make us some biscuits for supper, Glenda said. Her skirt had once been long enough but as she'd grown it rose until it barely touched her knobby knees. She was barefoot, her feet slim and pretty.

You need fire for biscuits, Phyllis said. Out the window a chipmunk twittered.

Yeah, Beckie said.

Where are the matches? Bobby said.

Beckie removed everything off the shelves, a set of rough dusty boards mounted to the wall by handhewn brackets. She piled the goods on the table. There wasn't much—the rusty pot from the shed, a pencil, a few sheets of paper, a jar one quarter full of salt, a brush, the iron spider. On the bottom shelf she had begun to keep the few ragged toys the littlest ones brought with them, a tin truck with three wheels, a blankface rag doll that Bev hauled around, Richard's bird book, a can of pebbles.

Beckie was in charge of numbers. It was Glenda's revelation, that without a calendar the days could run together, like colors in a washing, until everything was some nasty shade of brown, tarnished and filthy.

Every morning when you wake up, she'd said to Beckie. *Put a rock in this can. Every rock is one day. That's how we're gonna be able to keep track. You understand?*

Okay, Beckie had said although she didn't really understand.

Now Glenda poured the contents of the can into her hand. She counted quietly then shuffled the pebbles back into their holder.

How many? said Bobby.

Twenty-one.

They went back outside where the little kids were playing beside the stream. *I only know three ways to get fire*, Richard said, a decibel above the running water but not as loudly as a mourning dove calling from the shed roof. *One is lightning. Two is from somebody who has some. Three, matches.*

A wildfire, Bobby said. *That's four.*

But that came from lightning to start with, Glenda said.

Yeah, said Richard. *There is one other way. I saw a man at the Indian store do it. He was an Indian. He was hitting a rock against another rock.*

Really? Glenda said. She couldn't believe that.

84

I saw it, he said. *He had a pile of fluffy dry stuff, like thin cornshucks or dry moss, and he lit one tiny spark. I mean tiny. He kept feeding it, bigger and bigger things. Dry stuff. Finally it was a fire.*

Beckie chose a couple of handsize rocks, smooth and rounded, and knocked them against each other.

He did it like this, Richard said. He picked out two rocks and struck them against each other sideways, glancingly.

Nothing happened.

Maybe it has to be a special kind of rock.

May be.

The best thing to do is find the matches, Glenda said. *Either Ruby hid them or took them.*

Why do you call her Ruby? asked Beckie.

That's her name.

Her name is Mama.

I call her Mama, said Glenda, *most of the time. Don't you dare tell her different. I'll be right back.*

She conducted a thorough search of the partitioned off space that Ruby called her bedroom. She let out a whoop.

Come see, she hollered.

The children dropped their rocks and met her at the porch. She had a quart jar in her hand.

Preserves, she crowed.

Where did you find them?

In Mama's room.

Put them back, Phyl said.

Are you insane? Glenda said. *We're hungry. We are eating them.*

She'll whip you, Phyl said.

I don't care. What's a whipping? Better than starving to death.

I'm hungry, Beckie said.

She might kill you, Phyl said.

If she kills anybody, it'll be you, Glenda said.

Mid-morning found the children mixing pear preserves with flour and devouring the sweet brown paste.

We're saving half the jar, Glenda said. *For supper.* She knew they needed a plan. As the oldest, she and Bobby had to figure something out.

She got the younger children playing with the toy truck and the doll. Richard had passed the morning striking rocks against each other. Once Beckie saw a spark fly, or said she did.

We need to go for matches, Glenda said to Bobby, low.

Where? he said.

To the store.

How will we pay for them?

Maybe Mr. Fiveash has some work, she said.

Okay, he said.

Okay.

We better go now.

Okay.

Chapter 16

Bobby

All this brings back memories I don't want to think about. A person needs a mother and a father. They damn sure need somebody.

I have no love in my heart for my father either. My father was a selfish man. He didn't care what pain he caused my mother. He left her to raise eight children right by herself.

In my life, you know, I've heard lots of stories about bad things done to kids. Kids locked in rooms, in cages. Babies left on doorsteps. Big ones dropped off at orphanages. Kids left with grandparents. Kids sold to somebody else.

When you're young, your parents can do the most heinous things in the world and you don't see it. It's something weird in a kid. At the children's home a boy's pa had run over him with a truck, and when the boy talked about his father, it was in terms of great love and admiration. That boy would fight you over his father. You dared not say a bad word.

He tried to murder you, I told that kid one time.

You shut up, he said, and he punched me right in the mouth. *I mean it*, he said. *It was a mistake. He couldn't see me. He didn't mean to hurt me.*

It's only later, if you're lucky, that you start to see the truth.

Chapter 17

Fiveash proves to be of assistance.

This time Fiveash came out when his cur sounded. He stood a moment as the children approached. He was a heavyset man with a pipe hanging out of his mouth. He had a bushy mustache that dipped full down to his jaw. He speculated on them, turned away, and ducked inside.

Bobby pushed open the door, followed by Glenda. Phyl and Richard trailed behind them. The bigger kids had stashed the little ones in bushes back along the trail. They told Jimmy and Beckie not to move, to watch Bev and Jean. Beckie was four and started to holler but they shut her up.

We have to go first, Glenda said. *You can go later.*

The man, encamped behind his wooden counter, stood waiting for them. *How can I help you?* he asked, as if they'd been any customers in the world.

Are you Mr. Fiveash? Bobby asked.

Yes, sir, I am.

My name's Bobby. We need to build a fire and we don't have matches. We need matches. We need food too.

The woman had come to the front room from the back, wiping her hands on a gray apron lashed about her waist. Her hair twisted into its bun. *What's this all about, Mr. Fiveash?* she said.

They need a few things, the man said.

They need to go someplace else, she said.

Now, Mrs. Fiveash, don't be so quick to judge.

We don't need eight younguns to raise, she said.

Mr. Fiveash turned to Bobby. *Your mama's not up there, is she?*

No, sir.

I thought I saw her going down.

Yes, sir.

You younguns up there by yourselves?

Yes, sir.

Why do they want to do that?

I don't know. He added *sir* as an afterthought.

See what I say? Mrs. Fiveash said. *She's thrown out a whole sackful of runts. She's nothing but a lady of the night.*

Watch yourself, Mrs. Fiveash, said Mr. Fiveash. *Son, I'm pretty sure you don't have money and no way to get any. That right?*

Bobby nodded.

So if I hand you whatever you need how am I going to stay in business? It's "root hog or die" for all of us.

Could I do some work for you? We can all work. He thought of his smallest brother and sisters waiting in the bushes. *Most of us*, he said.

What kind of work can you do?

Whatever you need.

Can you chop wood?

Pretty good, yes, sir.

Tell you what, son, I'm going to give you two matches. This will be the last time I do.

Thank you, Mr. Fiveash. That's kind of you.

C.C. is your grandfather, correct?

Bobby nodded. *Yessir.*

I'll speak to him, Mr. Fiveash said. *Next time I see him. I'll tell him you don't have what you need up there.*

Thank you, sir.

As the children began the long climb, they heard the shrill voice of Mrs. Fiveash raised at her husband. *Look what you done started,* she hollered, followed by a quiet reply.

Bobby was carrying the matches in his pocket. He was scared of losing them and he kept checking to make sure they were there. He was scared too that sweat from his hands would ruin them.

I watched her make hominy, Glenda was saying.

Me too, Bobby said.

We can do it, she said.

The wind blew out the first match as soon as Bobby struck it. When the match went out as quickly as it lit, nobody said a word. He stared at the little pile of sticks and straw he'd piled up while Glenda was filling the kettle with corn and water.

Then Glenda stood up and walked some distance away, picked up an old pan that Jimmy had been playing with. She began to fluff dry hemlock needles and straw into it, as if preparing to scramble eggs. She piled small twigs next to the tinder.

The wind did that, Richard said.

The wind's an old meanie, said Beckie.

We better go inside, said Glenda.

Inside, she set the pan on the floor. *Wait a minute,* she said to Bobby. She ordered the young ones to get close, to tighten up against each other in a circle. She told Bobby to lean low.

Hold the match pointed downward, she said. *So the fire climbs it.*

I know that, he said.

I'm just making sure, is all.

When he struck the lone match he felt stress in every fiber of his small body. The match flamed, a small orange teardrop in a cavernous world, and Bobby touched it to dry hemlock. It flashed and he kept adding straw, then the tiniest of twigs. The twigs burned quickly and the little fire shrunk almost to nothing, but Bobby patiently added straw and twigs and bigger twigs until he had a pan of fire, as if it were something that could be eaten. He felt himself breathing again.

Gotta move it, he said.

The pan was already hot to the touch but he picked it up anyway, and so he turned, the circle of children breaking, and ran for the yard. He ran like an Olympian, his torch held low to his chest. He dropped the pan at the firepit and rushed to tend it, since the orange ball had become disheveled during the transport and because the fire was chewing quickly through the thin branches, leaving hollows of cooling ash before his eyes.

Inside, Glenda had moved back to the food shelf and was brushing her hand across the plank, feeling for something she might have missed, when she knocked a number of pebbles to the floor. They skittered in all directions.

That's my counters! wailed Beckie.

Hush, said Glenda. *Help me pick them up.*

But some went down the hole. Beckie started to cry.

Did they? Glenda asked the other kids.

I saw some go down, said Richard. *One or two.*

Beckie was still crying. *More than two.*

Richard moved to the edge of the rotten hole in the floor. *Too dark to see down there*, he said.

Hush, crybaby, Glenda said. *We'll get them back. Why didn't you have all the rocks in the can anyway?*

Those are the ones since Mama left last time, Beckie gulped. *Now we don't know.*

The children scoured the floor, handing pebbles to Beckie, quartz and mica and feldspar, although they did not know these names. Beckie was at eight stones.

Here's one, said little Jimmy.

Nine.

The children were quiet.

And you think two went down the hole?

One or two, Glenda said, shrugging.

That evening they ate the bloated kernels of corn before it had become hominy. Then Bobby remembered something. He went inside and picked up an empty croker sack.

I'll be back, he said to Glenda.

Where are you going? she said. When her brother didn't answer, she said, *It'll be night soon.*

I'll be back.

He crossed the log that served as a viaduct and made his way down the narrow mountain trail. In places trees had fallen and there were logs to climb. He came out on the far side of Grover's pasture and began to hike around it, clinging to the tree line. Dusk was falling and the red cows were lowing. Somewhere somebody kin to him was probably milking one of those cows and the thought of milk made his mouth water. Through a fringe of hemlock down in the holler he saw a lantern bobbing toward the large gray rectangle of what would be the barn. He moved furtively and surely.

He could smell the tree before he got to it, around it rising the sweetness of the first stages of rot. He had to cross a split-rail fence and then he was directly at it. In the last glimmers of day he could see red globes hanging. He began to pick, peering among the rough branches for the largest fruits. He wanted badly to eat one.

He heard a scraping noise near the house and then someone's voice unfurled into the night. It was his aunt, Meryl, calling Virgil, her oldest son, his first cousin. In response, one of the mules in the mule-pen brayed, a long hiccup that made Bobby, even in his furtiveness, smile. He slipped next to the trunk of the apple and quietly lowered his sack into the long grass. The apple seemed ancient, its bark rough and pitted, intent on creating bristly twigs and stobbing them with fruit. Bobby could feel the placidity of the tree.

Virgil answered, lantern in his hand. *Coming, Mama*, he called. A door closed with a meaningful thud.

Bobby waited, still as a predator. A chicken cackled out into the darkness, jostling on its roost. Now the lantern in the distance began its voyage across the clearing and soon was gobbled up by the house.

Bobby had to hurry. He grabbed at apples, dropping them wildly into the sack. A mellow honey-smell rose from them, and his mouth watered. His sack wasn't heavy enough when a dog started to bark. He lifted the sack and hopped back across the fence, then began running along the treeline, bee-lining through the grass of the darksome pasture. The red cows had moved and he was running toward them, and they, spooked, galloped away, except for a large red one that Bobby realized had to be a bull. Bobby raised his free arm, making low growling sounds, squaring with the bull, which wheeled heavily on his back legs and followed the herd.

Bobby found the opening to the trail in the dark and threaded his way across the mountain, fighting brambles that reached out long arms to scratch him. He shifted the sack of apples from one hand to the other as he ran. At the creek he picked his way across the viaduct and soon he was home.

Chapter 18

Bobby

For the rest of my life, an apple meant something to me. It was a trigger, really, but in a good way. Any apple at all would bring back that moment. In the darkness of the cabin the kids had reached into the sack. I took one, the biggest I could feel. I put mine immediately to my mouth and bit into it. My mouth flooded. It was like I'd been fasting for a week and finally God had handed me the sweetest food in the world.

The flesh was sugary, with a flavor like vanilla and cinnamon mixed together, and it sent runnels of juice down the corners of my mouth. I concentrated on one side of the apple and began to eat my way around the globe, finally devouring the calyx end and then the core, swallowing seeds and all, saving for the last bites the chalice of the stem end. I fished the thick stem from my mouth.

Breakfast the next morning had been apples, as had been many meals to follow. In the morning light the skin of the apple was red with golden tones, a kind of russet. That day Beckie sat and polished every apple until it shined.

For most people, apple pie is a comfort food, and they hold some sweet memory of it, warm and tender from the oven, apples thick with brown sugar and flour, floating in butter within the warm pocket of crusts, one across the bottom, and the other, decorated with a cut-out pastry star, across the top. It would be years before I ever tasted apple pie, and the feeling I would get from it would be sadness more than comfort.

All my life, a good mountain apple would thrill me, truthfully. A good apple was a thrill.

I became a familiar of that tree at Grover's and of many more like it in the months and years to come, until all the apple trees in the holler were laid down on a map in my mind. I knew the trees intimately, following them like bees from bare limbs in January to greening in May, to blossom-time also May, to green apples in July and August, to the rich redolence of ripening fruit along about October. I would compare apple flavors and frequent my favorites. No tree would ever be as joyful to me, not even a Christmas tree.

To this day I could draw you an atlas of the apple trees that grew up Loving.

Chapter 19

A day equals more than a pebble.

The next morning as soon as he woke, before all the others, Bobby bent and looked down the hole. The other children had told him about the pebble catastrophe. The ground below the floor was carpeted with rocks as if the mountain, in an attempt to wash the shanty away, had scoured the earth and left its bones showing. Hearing her brother up, Beckie crawled off the straw pallet with a loud autumnal rustling, pausing to wipe her eyes and to lift from the tick a dirty rag doll, which she tucked under one elbow.

How many's down there? she whispered. She was wearing the same dress, dirty and stained, she'd worn the day before and the day before and the day before that.

No way of knowing, he said.

Then he turned and went out the front door, opening the bottom half, Beckie following, the two of them greeted, as usual, by the ruin of the porch. They stood for a minute on the planks left intact, then delicately crossed a joist each, balancing barefoot across the gauntlet of timbers. Bobby leapt to the ground, and Beckie picked her way down the steps, which had four or five runners where there should have been seven or eight. Bobby disappeared around back of the house, and Beckie made her way to a tree where she pulled up her dress and squatted. A few minutes later both of the children were hunkered by the rock-lined stream, splashing water from cupped hands onto their faces, then drawing handfuls up to drink.

The creek never stopped running and it gave them all the water they wanted. The creek talked to them in quiet, concerned tones. The creek bathed them and played with them.

Why do you call your doll Beckie? said Bobby.

That's her name.

That's your name.

It's her name too. Beckie glanced at her doll, which she had leaned against a ham-sized rock. One button eye was missing. *She needs a house.*

This can be her house, offered Bobby.

Where?

Right here. This is the kitchen. Bobby hefted a rock and put it down, then another, setting them down in a line until he had a square drawn with rocks. He got to his feet and ranged streamside, coming back with a small, flat-sided stone. *This is the table*, he said.

Beckie watched him. He placed four little chairs around the table. *We need an icebox,* she said, and her eyes set on a granite hunk that looked nothing like an icebox. She relocated her icebox to the kitchen and pretended to open its door.

Now, children, she said in a high, chirpy voice. *We have bread and here's butter and here's jam and here's some fried eggs and here's milk for everybody.* As she spoke she swiveled looking for pebbles and setting them on the table-rock. She brought her rag doll up to the table. The doll was an invertebrate and plunged headfirst into her breakfast.

Make the bedroom, Beckie said to Bobby.

Bobby outlined another square with rocks and piled pebbles up to look like a pallet.

Now eat all you want, Beckie said in her high voice. *Then it'll be time for bed and I'll tell you a story.*

Bobby got up.

Are you leaving? Beckie said.

He didn't answer. He walked to the dead ashes of the fire and kicked at them. The kettle was full of cold corn, swollen and barbaric. A couple of dead, curled leaves lay on top of the gruesome white kernels.

But I want you to play with me, Beckie called. *I like playing with you.*

I've got other stuff to do, he said. He had to figure something out.

That day he said to Glenda that they needed a meeting. Her eyes lit up and she clapped her hands, and for a minute he saw her as a schoolteacher, calling for order.

Where should we meet?

Right here, he said. They sat on the steps.

Meeting time, she called. *Phyl, let's go. Richard.* She began to round them up until finally all eight of them were close, seated on planks and rocks.

We have been left here, Bobby said. *Way out in the woods. We have to figure out how we're gonna get by.*

Left here? Beckie said. *Mama's not coming back?* She started to cry.

Stop crying, said Glenda. *She's coming back. But probably not today. Maybe not tomorrow. Why don't you take Jimmy and Bev over to the creek and show them Beckie's house?*

Phyl was sitting cross-legged on the ground, holding the baby. One side of her face was swollen from her mother's last visit. Ruby had begun yelling at Phyl the moment she arrived, then had removed a shoe and smacked her across the face with its high heel, hard. Phyl had crawled under the house to get away from her.

We've got to face the facts, Bobby was saying now. *We have to take care of each other and keep everybody safe. Plus winter is coming. We need a plan. First we need to think of what all we can eat.*

We still have corn, Glenda said.

I'm talking longterm, he said.

By the end of the meeting, they had decided to raid the apple tree again. They'd take some of the potatoes Bobby had seen in his uncle's field. Bobby would meander toward their grandfather's farm and see what he could find. Glenda and the little children would gather firewood. Glenda, who was her mother's pet, would ask for more blankets the next time Ruby came. She would find out what Ruby had done with the matches. They would visit Mr. Fiveash to inquire about work again. Phyl would take care of Baby Jean. They'd all take care of the little ones.

Bobby knew what he would have to do.

Chapter 20

Bobby

I didn't decide then that I was going to kill her. That came later.

Chapter 21

Bobby finds a smokehouse and root cellar that are not empty.

Every day seemed a little colder than the one before and now the children slept tightly wadded under their few quilts and blankets. Bobby was rambling daily, always with a couple of flour sacks bulging his pockets. He called it "hunting." *I'm going hunting,* he'd say to the other children. He found potatoes in a field at Grover's farm and brought home two sacks at a time. They had extra now.

Where do we put them? Glenda had said. *If Mama sees them…*She didn't finish her sentence.

Finally they decided to scoop a hole in a corner of the dirt-floored lean-to. Bobby kept a thin layer of straw over them.

While Glenda distracted Fiveash, Bobby had stolen a box of kitchen matches.

What's happening up there ain't none of my business, Fiveash was saying. *But it don't seem right.*

It's all right, Mr. Fiveash, Glenda said to him. *We'll get along.*

Somebody ought to do something. When I can get to town, I'm going to report it myself.

Report what? Glenda asked him.

The fact that all you younguns are up that mountain all by yourselves.

Mama comes when she can, Glenda said. *She comes a lot.*

Ever time she comes she has to pass right by my store, said Fiveash. *And unlessen she's coming and going in the middle of the night, I'm not seeing her.*

Bobby had reached the door, headed out. He pulled it open nonchalantly. Bobby thought he should say "thank you" or something, not just walk out like that, but that might seem suspicious.

Please don't report us, sir. They might take us away. And separate us, Glenda was saying.

I don't like it atall, the storekeeper grumbled. His mustache twitched at the bottom of the horseshoe.

See you later, Mr. Fiveash, Glenda said and followed Bobby out. He was fumbling with one of his sacks, which he handed to her.

Hold it a minute, he said, and stepped back inside.

Fiveash looked up. He had a cracker in his mouth and he chewed it as Bobby approached his counter.

Mr. Fiveash, Bobby said.

Fiveash swallowed with some difficulty. *What is it, son?* The tiniest specks of crumbs shot from his mouth.

There's an old apple tree at the edge of the woods, Bobby said.

Back out behind the johnnie? Fiveash brushed at his mustache.

Yessir.

That's an Arkansas Black, Fiveash said. *Best apple there is.*

Do you mind if I take some?

Fiveash knew that he couldn't sell apples. Everybody in the mountains had trees, and Eliza Fiveash could boil all day every day and not put up all the apples thrown by that old tree.

Fiveash glanced toward the closed door of his living quarters and lowered his voice. *Don't let Mrs. Fiveash see you*, he said.

After that, Bobby considered it a victory when he could sneak behind the store and take apples without the dog yapping. He learned the dog's name, Minnie, and after a while he and Minnie became friends.

In late October Bobby went to his grandfather at the edge of town. He found Mr. Allen and Hiram pulling corn off dry stalks in a field near the house, throwing husks and all into a wagon pulled by the jenny mule. Pet heard him before the men did, her immense ears straight up, flicking right and left like antennae. She turned her head to stare wildly at him and snorted air from her nose.

Mr. Allen looked up then. He watched Bobby struggle toward him through the plowed, rocky ground of the field.

What is it, boy? he said.

*I came to…*the boy hesitated.

Something happened to Ruby? the man demanded.

No, sir. Not that I know of.

Where is she?

I don't know, sir.

Then what are you doing here? Why ain't you-uns out looking for her?

We're needing some vittles, the boy said.

The man glanced toward the house and brushed his hands together. *Hiram, keep at it,* he said. *I'll be back directly.*

Bobby followed Mr. Allen across the field, stopping under a maple twenty feet from the house. At the house the man opened the door. *America,* he called from the stoop.

A short, heavy woman appeared. She was dark-skinned because, Bobby knew, she was part Cherokee. He also knew that she saw him waiting at the edge of the yard. She wore a lightblue patterned dress with thick stockings underneath and a flowered apron over the dress. The apron looked moist and wadded in places. Her eyes were dark and hard, her thin lips clamped like a wound.

America, the old man said. *Those children need some vittles.*

C.C., I've told you. I want no part of that.

We've got plenty, he said.

Where's Ruby? she asked.

He said he doesn't know.

Her lips disappeared. *He needs to find that daddy of his'n,* she said. She stepped back and shut the door, hard.

Allen made his way carefully back down the steps. He walked barefoot, as was his way. As long as weather permitted, he wouldn't wear brogans, and Bobby marveled that he could tolerate the cold ground.

You heard her, he said. The boy didn't know what to do. Should he say his partings and walk off down the road? Allen had started back to the field. Bobby stayed in step with his grandfather.

We're in need, he said. *The littluns is hungry.*

The old man stopped. *I can give you some roasting ears*, he said.

Thank you, sir. Even as Bobby said it, the words began to roar in his ears and stop up his head. Why should he thank the old man? C.C. Allen was letting his own grandchildren live in a shanty up a mountain, starving to death. Out of sight of the house Mr. Allen filled a croker sack with ears of dried corn.

You able to tote this?

Yessir, I can get it, Bobby said.

Two weeks passed and one day the kids woke to rain. Icy rain fell all day. Glenda got a fire going in the pot-bellied stove in the house and kept it going until the wood gave out. She had learned to parch corn, and she did so in the spider. Bobby went out looking for more wood and came in with armfuls, wet and dripping, and he piled the thin branches on the crumbling bricks of the hearth. About dark the rain stopped.

Sometime before midnight the baby's crying woke the children one by one in the freezing house. Phyl was trying to quiet her.

We need more wood on the fire, Glenda said. Her teeth clacked. She got up. *Can you light the lamp?* Ruby had brought up a kerosene lamp.

Bobby got up and shuffled to the table. He heard the stove door sing open and Glenda breaking and adding twigs. He was shivering.

It's freezing, he said.

Go get that quilt off Mama's bed.

Bobby moved painstakingly across the cabin, watching for the hole in the floor and running his hand along the wall to know where he was. He felt for the doorknob and opened the door. The room smelled like the ground underneath an oak tree but with a hint of perfume too. He groped his way to the bed and pulled off the quilt.

Glenda thought she heard something. *Listen,* she said. The baby was still wailing. *Phyl, can you get her quiet?*

She's wet.

Wrap her in this, Glenda said, handing her a shirt.

Something was hissing from the sky.

Can you tell if that's rain? Glenda said.

Bobby moved to an open window and stuck his arm outside, palm up. *Sleet,* he said. *Or ice one.*

Sleet is ice.

Then the sound deepened, and whatever fell from the sky clattered like rocks against the roof and Bobby knew the sleet had turned to hail.

When they knelt on the tick, Glenda said to all of them, *We've got to huddle closer.*

The children woke to snow on the ground, two inches of white powder covering everything and the shanty so cold their breaths came out like a language of clouds. Even that was nothing compared to what was to come.

Gather firewood today, Bobby said to Glenda. *As much as you can. Whatever you can find, pick up and bring it back. Stack it on the porch. I'm going hunting. I'll be gone awhile.*

Bobby was gone all day. When he got home he was carrying a loaded croker sack, which he lifted onto the shanty table.

That was heavy, he said.

Glenda took one look and crowed. *Is that a ham?*

Yes.

She leaned closer. *Where did you get it?* she whispered.

He didn't look at her. *I went all the way to Mr. Allen's again*, he said.

You did?

Yeah.

Did they see you?

I don't think so, he said. Glenda had grabbed the frying pan while Bobby emptied the rest of the sack on the table. *I saw smoke coming out the cracks of the smokehouse and so I sneaked in there. That's how I got it. It's not all the way smoked yet. I knew somebody would be checking on the fire so I got right out. Remember they have a pear tree where the apples are? I sneaked around there and got some pears and apples. The house was all shut up but I know people were in there. There was smoke coming out the chimney. I tried to keep something between me and the house, all the time. Look at this.*

What is it?

Pork sausage in corn husks.

Mrs. Allen would kill you.

Yeah, he said. He glanced at the little kids. *Damned old bitch.*

Yeah, she said. *Old bitch.* Glenda already held the rusty knife like a weapon and was hacking slices of meat from the ham, throwing them on the spider. *I'm so hungry I could eat this raw*, she said.

I wouldn't. Bobby picked up a pear and handed it to her. She took a bite then laid the pear carefully on the rough table, opened the stove door, and threw in some twigs.

I thought of something, she said.

What?

Your footprints? At Mr. Allen's? They sounded like questions.

Yeah, he said. *I didn't even try to scrub them out.*

They'll know you were there.

They'll know somebody was there, I guess.

Glenda took a deep breath and let it out slowly.

Now I know which corncrib they're filling, Bobby said. *And something else.*

What?

I found the root cellar.

What's in it?

Lots of stuff. Turnips. Rutabagas. Big jugs and crocks. Worlds of sweet potatoes.

The night was deep and a half-moon risen when the children heard both parts of the door open. Bobby woke up with a start and he could see Ruby outlined in silver. She clicked over to the straw tick.

Mama? said Bobby.

I'm not in any kind of mood, she said.

Phyl had half-risen from where she lay curled around Jean, Bev on the other side.

Suddenly Ruby strode to Phyl and grabbed her by the hair. Phyl gave a small gasp and shut off a squeal. *Nor from you, missy. You think you're something, prissing around with the babies acting like you're their daddy and you ain't nobody, just another son of a bitch.* She lifted Phyl by the hair and began to beat her with something in her hand, in the face.

Bobby jumped up. *Stop,* he yelled to his mother. *Stop it.*

All of the children were awake now, the two smallest crying.

You keep out of this, Ruby said. She lifted Phyl to her feet and dragged her across the room, then out the front door.

Take off your clothes, she said savagely. *You're not sleeping in the same house with me.*

A minute later she strode back into the house, Phyl's clothes in hand.

What are you doing? said Bobby. *You put her outside. And took her clothes. Are you out of your mind? It's freezing. She'll die out there.*

His mother was standing near the stove. The house was dark but there was enough light for her to pick up a long iron spoon. She hit Bobby straight in the mouth with it.

You don't watch it, you'll be next, she said.

Chapter 22

Bobby

After Ruby went in her room that night and the kids went back to
sleep, I tried to decide what to do. I sneaked to the door and looked
around for Phyl, but I couldn't find her. I didn't want my mother to
come find me at the door, so I tiptoed back to the mattress. I heard
shuffling under the house, and after that I heard Phyl crying, very
softly. I took off my shirt and dragged myself inch by inch to the
hole.

Phyl? I whispered.

She didn't answer.

I lowered my head farther in the hole, thinking about the
rattlers and Phyl under there. *Phyl,* I hissed.

Her answer was bare audible.

Here's some clothes, I said. *Try to get over here closer to the hole.* She
took the shirt and I passed a blanket to her.

But it wasn't that night that made me decide. It was the
sheriff coming. He came early the next morning. Maybe they'd had a
fight because he went into her room. Ruby came out and told us all
to get out of the house. There was a lot of yelling then things
quieted down then there were different kinds of noises, kind of like
oohing and ahhing and a little laughing.

When the sheriff left he cast a glance or two at us, walked to the edge of the clearing, turned his back, and peed in the bushes.

That day I started looking.

Chapter 23

Christmas passes unbeknownst and January almost brings disaster.

One day Bobby was passing the store when the door opened and Fiveash came out. He was wearing a bulky gray woolen coat and held a pipe in his hand, from which a thin worm of smoke twisted.

Hey, boy, he called.

Bobby stopped and turned back. *Yessir,* he called. His breath turned to cirrus in the cold air.

I need to see you, son, Mr. Fiveash said.

When Bobby stepped up, he saw that Mr. Fiveash had recently combed his hair. It was swept across the top of his head in little rows, like a dark plowed field. His coat had suffered attacks of moths, visible along the collar and the sleeves.

Son, your grandpa stopped by.

Yessir?

Well...

Bobby waited.

I tell you like this. You can come on in and get a few things.

Sir?

Your grandpa allowed me to tot a bill.

Today? Bobby said. *Right now?*

Yessir, Mr. Fiveash said. *Come on in and get what you need.*

Thank you, sir.

An hour later Bobby was back at the cabin. He went in the front door and set a heavy, clanking sack on the table.

Glenda rushed over first and looked in the sack. *Where did you get all this?* she asked in a whisper. *You stole it?*

No, he said, low. *I stopped by Mr. Fiveash's. He said Mr. Allen was going to let us charge.*

Glenda sat down abruptly on a makeshift chair. *Charge?* she said. *At the store?*

Yeah.

Charge means get things without paying for them.

It means getting things and Mr. Allen pays Mr. Fiveash later.

Glenda leapt up and began unsacking the food—tinned meat, sack of salt, bag of beans, another of rice. *Thank god almighty,* she said. *Sugar. Grits. Eggs. Coffee. He let you have coffee?*

I got it and he didn't say anything.

Why didn't you get us some candy?

There are a few things that we can't get.

We can't get candy?

No. And no sodas, no tobacco, no snuff.

Why in the world would any of us want snuff? We're hungry.

Maybe to keep from feeling hungry.

How often can we go?

He didn't say.

Maybe we're gonna be okay. But we need powder milk, she said.

Bobby looked at her.

For the baby, she said.

I'll be right back.

And kerosene.

How do I get kerosene?

In a can, she said. *Get some in this can.*

I'll never get back up here without spilling it.

Walk carefully, she said.

Bobby passed back out into the cold. He paused a moment on the porch, his eyes streaming. He wiped them and leaped to the ground. He was down the trail and up again in a jiffy. He was used to the mountain now. The mountain itself seemed to help him get down and back up.

That very day the baby had milk.

The children knew Christmas because on one of her visits Ruby said the word. But the way she said it was past tense. Glenda stopped and went up close to her.

When is Christmas?

Months away, Ruby said.

This Christmas is gone?

Ruby pressed her lips together. *Done gone,* she said. She glanced at her oldest daughter and in that glance was some brand of pity.

Glenda froze, statue of a young girl. Ruby had brought a couple more ragged quilts and a sack of clothes that church-ladies had given her. Most of the clothes had belonged to grown men and were worn and torn, threadbare in places, but the children were wearing them. The black dress Glenda snagged went to her calves and hung on her like a sack. Underneath it her hosiery was jangled with runs. Although Glenda tried never to show emotions, now at mention of a Christmas already passed her bottom lip quivered, and a single tiny tear squeezed out of the far corner of one eye. It didn't slide far. She turned her face away but Ruby had seen.

We'll do Christmas next year, Ruby said.

I don't care about no old Christmas, Glenda said. Her voice was bitter.

Later, after Ruby had gone, Glenda told the others that Christmas had come and gone. Some of them started to cry. *Santy Claus didn't bring us nothing*, Beckie said. *He forgot us way out here.*

Rain fell all one day. Bobby left in the rain. He descended to the store, but he couldn't get any food. Fiveash mumbled something about wanting to make sure he could get his money. Bobby made the hard climb back up, wet, shivering, dejected. Stick by stick the older children fed their supply of wood into the stove until dark fell.

We don't have enough covers for this, Bobby said.

We need to put on all the clothes we can, Glenda said. She ranged the cabin picking up anything she could and instructing someone to put it on. Beckie was wearing a grown man's pants. Phyl was rolling up the cuffs so that Beckie could shuffle about. Bev was wearing a woman's shirt, its sleeves rolled high.

I'll go look for wood, Bobby said.

It'll be wet, Glenda said.

Bobby came in some time later out of the darkness. The cabin was completely dark except for a small glow from the lamp and another from the cracks in the stove.

Did you find anything? Glenda said.

Not much, he said.

The children slept huddled in a wad. Sometimes in the night one or the other of them would wake up, shivering. Glenda would wake too.

Jimmy, stop pulling the covers.

Glenda, he wailed. *I'm cold.*

If you pull the covers you'll uncover the rest of us.

They already had the covers from Ruby's room and still they were freezing. From about midnight to daybreak Bobby lay awake, curled sideways around Jimmy. He owned an ill-fitting wool coat and he tried to keep it over the two of them. Toward daybreak the rain stopped and at dawn he donned his coat and went out into the day. The rest of the children heard him dumping sticks on the porch.

The temperature was dropping steadily. By ten the day was colder than it had been at nine. Bobby told Glenda to try to keep the fire going.

Everything is soaking wet, she said.

Lay it all around the stove and try to dry it out, he said.

I'm trying, she said.

That evening the fire was a pitiful gray nest of embers when the children, who had been driven by dropping temperatures deeper into a huddle, tried to sleep. Supper had been cold hominy and they were freezing.

The children woke to Phyl screaming. *The baby's dead*, she was saying. *The baby's dead*. In their sleep the children had clawed toward each other, pushing the baby out to the perimeter of their knot and finally out from under the blankets. Instead of mewling, she had slowly succumbed to cold.

The moon was some days past full, and it was high and bright in the sky.

Where is she? Bobby said.

Phyl was sitting up on the straw tick, holding the baby close to her flat chest and wailing. *She's dead*, she kept moaning.

Let me see, said Bobby.

The baby's face was blue, Bobby could see that even in moonlight. He touched her. The skin of her head was icy. Her little arms were stiff and icy. But he could see the slightest puff of air coming from her tiny nostrils.

She's not dead, he said. *But she's going to be if we don't get her warm.*

Lay down, he said to Phyl, and wrap around her. Then he had Bev and Jimmy curl into Phyl and Beckie into Bev and Richard into Jimmy and then he and Glenda covered them all with the blankets that were like large leaves with worm holes eaten in them, and they slid in at the edges.

Breathe on her, Phyl, he said. *Glenda, you pray.*

Dear God, Glenda started. Her voice was tight and wavery with cold and came out muffled from the blankets. Bobby could tell she was shivering. *Dear God, we-uns are in a fix. We are cold and we need your help. We need it right now. Our little sister is about to die from being so cold. If you can help us I'll do my best to be a better person. Please save Jean. We don't have anybody but each other and we don't want to lose any of us.*

She had started to weep. She quit talking. A few minutes later she ended her prayer with a kind of chant, *Please God. Please God. Please God.*

You did good, Bobby said. *Just say amen now.*

Amen, she said.

After a silence while the moon poured its cold January juice all over them, and any warmth from its light ran out through the cracks in the room, Glenda said, *Bobby?*

Huh?

What do you think is going to happen to us?

We can't run out of wood any more, he said.

After that, the children, shivering with cold, spent hours every day stockpiling sticks, broken branches, rotted logs, and anything they could find that would burn. They visited the old log barn, pulled logs from its walls, and dragged them home. They piled wood in the house and on the porch, and when those places were full they stacked piles of sticks in the yard. Bobby took Jimmy with him and gathered wood like a madman. He rigged up a croker sack with a rope as a flat tote and filled it over and over, ranging farther and farther from the shack, fanning in all directions, dumping his loads and heading out again.

In the woods he looked for food. He found hickories and had Jimmy, wearing socks as mittens to tolerate winter, gathering hickory nuts while he filled the wood tote. Often he went back alone to the hickories with a sack and gathered every nut he could find. He gathered until his hands turned red and stung from the cold, and he had to stick them into his armpits to warm up.

He found mockernuts and he gathered them. He found a horse apple and he stripped what frozen fruit, all of it hard and bug-bitten, that was left.

He seemed to be looking for something else too. He'd pick up rocks, one by one, hold them a minute, and then set them down again. During those bitter January days Bobby must have considered a thousand stones.

One day when Ruby was home the boys had gone to the old barn to bring back planks. Suddenly from that direction came a terrific noise of cracking and falling.

Somebody's hurt, Glenda hollered. She started running.

Ruby grabbed Jimmy and began to trail Glenda along the stream path. The other children followed. Ruby got to the viaduct and was halfway across the icy, slippery beam when she set Jimmy down. She kept running. The water in that spot ran three feet deep and fast through a small gorge, and Jimmy sat motionless on the beam where Ruby had left him, terrified to move. The cold mountain water roared beneath him. When Phyl, slowed by the other small children, got to the viaduct, she balanced herself and crossed to him. She carefully picked him up and carried him across.

The entire barn had collapsed. Luckily none of the children had been inside the barn when it fell, and all were accounted for.

Somehow the children made it through January, February, and then March. Spring came slowly. Snow melted in the high places and one day Bobby came upon a patch of what he'd heard called trailing arbutus. It was a plant that grew close to the ground and now bloomed with pretty pink flowers. He noticed buds coming out along the bare white limbs of beeches. A patch of mayapple appeared, dangling white flowers beneath lobed leaves. Birds began more commonly to sing, and soon dogwood blooms looked like white boats floating on the green waves of the forest.

One day on the back flank of the mountain he noticed a wet patch of ground growing with something he recognized. He had seen these gathered when he was a young boy, before they had gone to Michigan. He had been with his mother when she had gone with her mother deep into the woods, his grandfather driving the wagon, and they had pulled out tall green plants with spiked leaves that smelled like onions.

Ramps.

Smelling them now, his tongue got slick. Bobby filled his sack.

Not long after he found the ramps the children found poke salat. They had all trailed down the mountain, mainly to look at the road. If they could see the road, then they would know that their mother might come to them again, because the road still led in one direction to where she was and then back in the other direction to where they were. If they saw Fiveash's store, and even Mr. Fiveash, they would know that all the world had not abandoned them.

How it happened was that down the mountain in what appeared to be an old field, Glenda spotted lots of reddish-green leaves sprouting from the cold, wet ground.

You-uns come look, she said, somewhat breathlessly. *This is poke salat.*

Bobby was never without his sack. *Start picking*, he said to her. *We can see the road tomorrow.*

A few minutes later he looked up to see Jimmy chewing on a leaf.

Spit that out, he said. *Right now. You can't eat it like this. It's poison.*

Jimmy spat.

Don't eat it like this, Bobby said. *It can kill you dead. We have to cook it first.*

Three times, Glenda said.

On the hike home Glenda said something about his sack. *What do you have in there? Something heavy. All that's not leaves.*

A rock I found, he said.

Sometimes on his travels Bobby would wind up at a little woods church below Bootleg Mountain called Pleasant Gap Tarplay Chapel. The whitewashed church sat on rocks in a yard made mostly of moss. It was a peaceful place and he liked sitting in the moss and plantain at the edge of the clearing, looking at the church, with nobody around. Sometimes he meandered among the graves in a little graveyard behind the church, reading the names: *Chastain, Sosebee, Smith.* One man named Johnson had been born in 1851 and had died in 1939. He lay beneath a double marker, although his wife's side only had a birth day, not a death day. "We were welded together," the marker said.

One day when he went by Pleasant Gap Tarplay men were digging a grave. Bobby sat on a downed hemlock a way off the road and watched. The last time he'd been through, there had been a drought and the road was dusty. Now it was damp, the trees were green, and the mountain laurel hung with clusters of pink bloom, like little cakes, frosted with sugar icing and frilly.

Down in the cemetery the ground was rocky, and every few minutes he would hear a shovel hit a rock with a clang. After a while people started to arrive, going mostly by twos into the church. He thought he recognized Mr. Allen among them, but he couldn't be sure. From his distance he couldn't hear anything, but after an hour of preaching and singing six men brought out a wooden coffin and they lowered it by ropes into the ground. By then a woman was wailing hard, and if he hadn't known better, he would have mistaken it for his own mother wailing, and the sound even at a distance was unbearable to Bobby, so he abandoned the damp hemlock and headed on up the mountain, back to where he'd come from, to the place where he and his sisters and brothers were welded together.

Chapter 24

Bobby

I am pretty sure they put us there to die. Mine could have been one of the graves dug at Pleasant Gap Tarplay. Very near my grave could have been Jeannie's, if she had frozen to death, or Jimmy's, if he had fallen off the viaduct. (That was Jimmy's first memory, by the way, of clinging to that ice-slick log while angry water seethed and clacked below.)

I've thought about this from all angles and that's what I come back to, every time. I think they needed to get rid of us and they were too proud to give us away, or maybe they didn't know anybody who would want us, and so they took us up that mountain to die. They figured the littlest ones would die first. And they almost did.

I made something out of my life. But through it all I carried this hard thing inside me, that I had been put away, that my own mother could not find something beautiful enough inside or outside of me to want to keep me, until finally I had to have a fake mother, which means that I never had a mother at all, and I have felt the unworthiness riding hard within me. It never would let go, even after I had my own family and my own business and my own kids and plenty of money. I had a rose garden with all variety of roses, and the roses I grew were larger, prettier, and more fragrant than those in Will's mother's rose garden. I had started to collect apples that would grow in the heat and humidity of southern Georgia, with names like Anna and Mattamuskeet. They ripened early in the summer, and that was my favorite time of year. Roses were blooming and apples were ripe.

It took me fifty years to even begin to look at this. Nobody talked about it except that one time, that Thanksgiving. I kept turning away from it and it kept trying to make me look. Then one day it grabbed me and I couldn't turn from it. We lived out in the country in a house we built for ourselves, my second wife and I, and I got on the golf cart and rode down to the pond I had dug, so I'd have a place to feed fish and watch the blue herons wading.

I didn't want to cry but I couldn't stop. Tears were running down my face. I'd wipe some off and as soon as I did, there would be more to mess me up. I knew I had to get ahold of myself. I sat there for a long time, unable to see anything in front of me except this watery wall like a windshield, my eyes just like a windshield in a rainstorm and me wiping constantly. My heart was hurting so bad. I sat there until I heard my wife back up at the house ringing the old school bell I had put up. I got out the rag I use to dust off the golf cart and I blew my nose good and swabbed at my face. I stood up and took a deep breath and dusted myself off, as if I'd been in a fight and I'd gotten my ass kicked, and it was going to take me a few days to not feel bruised and busted.

I made a phone call that night to my sister Phyl. She had received the worse end of it. I still can't deal with that part of the story. I wasn't strong enough to think about that, not the moment I'm talking about, and probably I never will be that strong. By then Phyl was divorced although she was still working at Publix. She worked there all her life, in the bakery department. On the phone I asked Phyl if she would come visit me and she said yes.

I knew that if she was here to back me up, I could tell my story.

Chapter 25

The children play a game of baseball.

Boys against the girls, Bobby said. *Me and Richard and Jimmy against Glenda and Phyl and Beckie.*

> *What about the babies?* said Phyl.

> *Leave them on a blanket yon*, said Bobby, who had set out stones from the creek in the shape of a rickety diamond.

> *You're on first*, Bobby said to Jimmy. *That's not first. It's the one over by that tree. Richard, you're on second. Back there by the path. I'll pitch.*

> *You don't have anybody on third,* said Glenda.

> *No*, said Bobby. *It's not perfect.*

A stout straight limb served as a bat, and the cone of a white pine was the ball. The pitcher's mound was only eight feet from home plate. Beckie went first, managed to punt the cone to the right of Bobby, and Glenda helped her run to first. She barely beat Bobby getting there.

Phyl stepped up and took the limb, but she swung wildly and after three strikes, she handed the bat to Glenda. Glenda had good aim and she was determined, and when she hit the cone it flew past Bobby. He ran to get it, yelling at Richard to get back to his base and get ready for the ball.

When the cone hit Richard, the child screamed and turned his attention to his arm, which had been scratched. He started to cry.

I'm sorry, Bobby said. *I was trying not to hit you.* Now Bobby was running to retrieve the cone because Glenda had picked up Beckie at first and was circling the bases, ignoring Richard.

The girls had three points before they had three outs, and then when the teams switched and the boys came in to bat, Bobby could hit and run the bases with ease. He met with no resistance in Beckie and Phyl and not much in Glenda. Richard had quit crying and could manage a hit. After five points Glenda called it quits.

Good game, she said. She trudged to the steps.

We need a real ball, Bobby said.

It'll work better when the little kids are bigger, she said. *Remember that game Daddy took us to?*

Yeah, Bobby said.

Remember the hotdog?

Yeah. With mustard on it. We ate it off the ground.

Yeah. What's wrong with that?

Nothing.

I'd like to have one now.

Bobby was quiet. *And popcorn all in the grass,* he said.

That one lady, Glenda said.

Yeah.

She was fancy. She was even wearing gloves. White gloves. Whatever happened to that dime she gave you?

Mama found it, he said. *I don't know what she did with it.*

You know what we could do with a dime now?

I'd spend it on every kind of candy in Mr. Fiveash's store. And a Co-Cola for everybody.

That would be nice, she said.

That day Jimmy lost one of his shoes. Nobody noticed at first because he walked home barefoot. When they realized, the next day, they were scared a little, because Ruby had only recently brought the shoes up the mountain. They looked under the straw tick and in Ruby's room. They looked down the hole in the floor. They looked all over the yard.

They were right to be scared. Ruby was angry when she arrived and found out, and she threatened to beat them all.

Why did you take them off? Ruby said to Jimmy.

They hurt, he said.

You'uns got to find it, she said.

That shoe could be anywhere, Bobby said.

It can't be far, said Ruby. She stopped. *You-uns aren't rambling, are you? I mean you to stay right around this cabin when I'm not here.*

No, ma'am, we're not rambling, Glenda said.

You find the shoe, Ruby said to Bobby, *and I'll give you a dollar.*

Bobby went out. He checked the creek and around the house, on to the rock outcrop. He thought about the baseball game and he went down the mountain to the cleared area where they had set up a diamond. No shoe. Any old raccoon could have dragged the shoe off into a hollow tree.

He traced back toward the cabin. He could follow the path they had come, around trees and past rocks and through timothy still wrinkled with their passage. And there it was, a small black shoe dropped in last year's leaves.

Found it! he said when he popped back in the door of the cabin. His brothers and sisters looked up, but they looked more scared. He could feel that something had changed.

Where's Phyl? he asked.

Nobody said anything.

Where's Phyl? His voice had risen.

Hand me the shoe, Ruby said. *Come here, Jimmy. If you wear these, after a while they won't hurt your feet.*

You give me the dollar, I'll give you the shoe, Bobby said to his mother. He had taken a few steps toward her.

Ruby looked at him, her eyebrows raised. Now he could look level into her eyes although he didn't like to look into them. He wanted to see something that was not there.

You didn't really think I was going to give you a dollar, did you? She snickered, holding out her hand for the shoe.

Suddenly a cauldron inside him began boiling up, as if bicarbonate of soda had been dropped into it. Whatever liquid the cauldron held slipped over a red-hot edge and dropped into a snapping fire, exploding into steam. In a kettle inside him, something was foaming over, bursting with loud pops, feeding an inferno. He slapped his mother's hand away.

What the hell do you think you're doing? she said. She came at him and grabbed the shoe, hit him across the temple with it.

She shouldn't have done that. Whatever filled the cauldron inside Bobby caught fire, and all of him went up in smoke. He drew back his fist and caught her on the left shoulder, just above the heart. She staggered backwards as he advanced, beating her. *You don't care about us. You only care about yourself. You wish we would all just disappear. What other kids have to live like this? You're not my mother. I don't know what you are but you're not our mother.* Bobby knocked Ruby to the floor.

A red membrane slid over his eyes, between the cornea and the eyelid, like a curtain of blood. It blinded him. He got his hands around her neck.

Ruby clawed at him with her fingernails. He could feel her red-painted nails slicing and scraping through his flesh. He squeezed his hands tighter around her neck. He felt her teeth, sharp and awful, on his forearm. They punctured his skin and bit into the muscle there. He felt himself trying to breathe, trying to get air into his lungs.

That's when he realized the little kids were screaming. He heard Richard wailing, high and disconsolately. *No, Bobby, no*, Richard wailed. *Don't hurt Mama*. The red curtain flew back up into whatever recess it had come from. Glenda had his head in her elbow, twisting hard. He loosened his grip on Ruby and flung Glenda away.

That was the day the tables turned.

Chapter 26

Bobby

I stole a lot of things when my brothers and sisters and I were up in the woods with nobody to look after us. Mostly I stole rations. I stole from my grandfather and from my uncle. I stole from Fiveash. I stole whenever I could. I even stole food, a lot of canned goods, from the school in Loving a few times. I learned how to go up under it and come in through a vent in the floor. I tried to replace things like they had been, so nobody would nail boards tight or add deadbolts to doors. One time I overheard my Aunt Meryl call us "thieves." I feel bad about all that. But is it stealing if it saves your life? If it saves the lives of your little brothers and sisters, is it stealing? I don't think so. I don't think there's any law in heaven about little kids stealing so they can live. Except stealing was not the worst of it.

Chapter 27

A year passes before a busybody from town pays a visit.

Ruby had stayed away a long time after Bobby tried to choke her to death. The bigger kids stashed the little kids in the bushes and went back to Fiveash's. He said it hadn't been long enough, they'd have to wait for the new month. He said to make a list and he'd get up what they needed. Beckie's tin can was long since abandoned, but again they started keeping better track of time, Glenda remembering the ditty that went "Thirty-one days has January…"

When Ruby finally came she didn't stay the night. Bobby reckoned that she only stopped by to see if they were still alive. She wasn't there twenty minutes before she went back down the trail. The kids had a fire going and they were cooking hominy. Ruby caught Bobby by the fire.

I've been staying at Anderson's Tourist Court, she said. *They give me a deal by the month.*

He wondered why she was telling him. He knew Anderson's. He remembered the sign, "Your Home Away from Home." Bobby looked off into the fire. In one field of his vision he could see the flames, and in another he could see the hotel where his mother was staying, while her poor children moldered away in a shanty in a mountain holler, and in even another field of vision he could see far away into the future. It looked dark, murky with stars.

Bobby, I know you and me have our problems, his mother was saying. *But this is no place for you. I've decided you're coming down and living with me in Morganton. You can git a job there. The copper mine's always hiring.*

Bobby stared at his mother. She wore a soft pink lipstick, a perky and stylish navy-blue hat on her head. The hat made her look as if she owned a million dollars.

His mind had clamped around her words and examined them from all vantages. She wanted to bring him to town, away from all the little kids. He understood very clearly. He also understood that she had made it sound like an order.

In another lifetime, Bobby would have to do what Ruby ordered. But this was a new lifetime and hers was not an order. It was an offer.

I'm not leaving, he said.

Dewberries came and went. Blackberries came. Ruby showed up once in a while, and she sometimes stayed a night and sometimes she didn't. Now the children had been living mostly alone in the woods for a year. One day deep into another fall Phyl heard something outside. *Shhhh*, she said.

Everybody got quiet.

Yoohooooo. Someone was calling from the path. *Anybody home?*

The children leaped for the door. Phyl set the baby on one hip and grabbed Bev by the hand. Fifty feet away, a lady with short white hair and silver glasses picked her way toward the cabin from the direction of the store. She was wearing black lace-up boots, a light-green skirt falling to her shoes, with a shorter dark-green skirt atop the lighter one. Nobody said a word. Glenda turned and shut both partitions of the front door behind them, and they all stood on the broken porch and watched as the lady moved closer through the weeds.

Hello, she said, too brightly. *You-uns live way up here. I was beginning to think I'd taken the wrong trail.* She flipped her skirt and looked down at her wet boots. *I hope I don't git dew pizen.*

Nobody said anything.

I've come to see your mother. Is she home? The question sounded both like consolation and a veiled challenge.

Glenda spoke then. *Yes, ma'am,* she said. *She's here. But she's sleeping. Can we help you?*

No. I'd like to see her.

The children were silent.

You-uns got everything you need?

Yes, ma'am, pretty well.

Run tell your mama I'm here. Carolina Auberry.

We don't dast wake her up, Glenda said. *She says when she's resting we should never wake her up, not for any reason.*

I can wait awhile, the woman said.

Glenda was silent. Mrs. Auberry walked on up to the porch, sat down on one of the front steps, and looked around. After a while she asked, doubtfully, *Yore'n'ses house is kindly cobbled up, ain't it?*

Nobody spoke.

You-uns okay up here?

Yes, ma'am.

Where's your outhouse?

We don't have one, said Glenda.

You got a gyarden?

No, ma'am.

Chickens?

No, ma'am.

Suddenly it hit Bobby that they needed a garden. Why had he not thought of it? He spoke up for the first time. *Can you have a garden if you don't have a hoe?*

Well, I reckon you could, the woman said. *You'd have to grapple in the ground with your hands. Course you'd need seeds.*

Bobby had forgotten seeds.

But seeds ain't hard to come by. Most everything et is full of seeds. You save yrself a few. The lady picked up her arm clothed in a long-sleeved, puffy brown blouse and pointed downhill, toward a patch of ground where the sun hit hard. *Yon would be a pretty good place for a gyarden. You could grow rimptions of taters and beans there.* She was quiet a minute. *Yes, I think you could git a heap of garden sass. I seed people grow in worse places.*

Once she had rested, the lady sent Glenda in to see if Ruby had awakened. Glenda went inside and shut the door, returned and shut the door, and reported that Ruby had not.

Well, I best git going since I'm footin it. Tell her Mrs. Carolina Auberry came by. She knows me. Tell her I came to check on her.

Yes, ma'am, said Glenda.

The lady stopped. *Tell her all you-uns are invited to Sunday meeting at Loving Baptist Church.*

Yes, ma'am.

Even before Mrs. Auberry was out of sight Beckie disappeared into the house. When she came back she said, *No, Glenda. Mama is not here.*

I know, said Glenda.

Why did you tell the lady she was here?

It was better, Glenda said.

But it wasn't true.

You want them to take us away from here? If I say that Mama's not here, they'll take us far away from here and we might never get to see each other again.

Beckie was quiet. Then she said, *I wouldn't go.*

You'd have to if they said so.

The way life haunts us sometimes, the children were exposed as liars, because not an hour later they heard their mother hollering from the trail for them to come help her. She was lugging some sacks up the hill.

A lady came this morning, Glenda said. *Mrs. Carolina Auberry.*

I just saw her, Ruby said.

She stopped a minute to catch her breath. The last of the blackberries were turning dark in a mound of brambles by the trail. As soon as one ripened, it was eaten. Over toward the creek, jewelweed had started to hang out its fiery pendants.

What did you tell her? Ruby asked.

We told her you were in the house, asleep, said Glenda.

Old bitch, Ruby said.

She stayed a night and was gone again.

Bobby was rambling. He always carried his sack and would come home with something, but equally important to the children were the stories. Sometimes he caught a ride down to Morganton, to Lake Blue Ridge. He would stand on the steel bridge between the boat dock and town, looking off at the still silver-blue water crowding up against the soft green mountains. He would walk down to the shoreline and if the weather was warm he'd jump in. Sometimes he'd fish, and when he did, he would come home with trout in his sack.

Sometimes he walked Allen Street in Morganton, pretending to own one of the large houses along it.

Sometimes he went toward Mineral Bluff or Blue Ridge. This is how he saw Wishon Livery Stables and Mineral Bluff Bank, mules tied to hitching posts out front. He saw Blue Ridge Drug Store and Blue Ridge Colored School. This was how he also saw a covered bridge across Hemptown Creek on Outcane Road, just outside Mineral Bluff.

He started hitchhiking, which is how he acquainted himself with surrounding communities—Hemptown, Hot House, Higdon, Deep Gap, Dial, and Fry.

One day he was in Blue Ridge when the train pulled in to the depot, a sight he described to his sisters and brothers in great detail. He was a few blocks away when he heard the train whistle. People started running in one direction, he said, and he started running with them. Soon he arrived at a depot, a long wooden building with a little room that stuck out toward the tracks. That was where an attendant could look down the tracks, watching for a train.

This train, now, was a magnificent beast, like a mad, metallic ox, pulling a string of heavy cars behind. It huffed right up to the station, panting. Bobby had no idea how a thing so enormous and powerful got itself stopped, but it did. A man in a uniform with a red hat levered a door open, and passengers began to step down off the train, holding valises and hat boxes and lunch sacks. They were well-dressed people, for the most part. Some of them stood train-side looking around at Blue Ridge, and some were met by cars from the big wooden hotel out on the lake. These folks had come to the mountains for a vacation. Pretty soon a whistle blew, loud and insistent, from the engine car, and the people waiting by the tracks toed up to the door of the train and climbed back inside. As the train pulled out, headed toward Atlanta, the people sitting by the windows stared out at Blue Ridge, unwaving.

The children remembered when they themselves had stared out at small towns, listening to the train whistle blow, unwaving.

Sometimes Bobby stopped in at the Loving Post Office, where he met the postmistress, Mrs. Susie Hunt, who wore round spectacles and long braids pinned around the crown of her head. Sometimes he turned north instead of south from Loving, toward Oak Grove Church. He walked the cemetery, reading names of people he did not know, Davenports, Auberrys, Rapers, Beavers. He would whisper the names out loud, Mammie Dills, Cloyce Queens. Occasionally he did not go down to Morganton at all, but launched himself in the other direction, and sometimes he got to the state line and crossed out of Georgia altogether and into North Carolina, although there was no sign and he remained ignorant of that geography until he was grown, had left the state entirely, and knew that he had.

He told his siblings about the funeral he'd seen at Pleasant Grove Tarplay, how one lady in a long black dress had tried to open up the box and grab the person inside. A bunch of people stopped her. She had hollered for a long time but finally she got quiet and the preacher said some things, kind of quickly, and some women took the hollering woman off into the church. The men lowed the casket into the ground with ropes and then got dirt back on the grave.

Reckon it took a while to dig that grave, said Bobby.

Six feet is deep, said Glenda.

Some Allens are buried at that church, Bobby said.

Ruby was an Allen, Glenda said.

You should call her Mama, Beckie said.

I do, said Glenda.

Not all the time.

In fact, we're kin to Tarplays, Glenda said. *One of them married an Allen. Maybe that's our church too.*

We don't have a church, said Richard.

They almost had the grave dug when I came up on them, Bobby said.

Who was it died?

I couldn't tell.

I wish we could go to church. That from Beckie.

They are footwashing Baptists, Bobby said.

How do you know? said Glenda.

Bobby had seen the service that involved feet-washing. That day he'd been so close he could look down from the road into a window. He said he could see a woman with her stockings off, her feet in a bucket of water. Other women kneeled around the bucket. At the back of the church, men were washing men's feet.

The children discussed why people would wash each other's feet at church. That was something they couldn't understand.

More months passed. Nobody knew the exact date, not even Glenda. By now the older children had grown accustomed to their lot in life, and they knew what they need to do to survive—they had to constantly seek food in whatever form they could find it, they had to stockpile firewood, they had to teach the little ones what they knew. Beckie, then Jimmy, learned to read from an old Sally, Jane, and Dick primer.

Birthdays slipped by unnoticed. One day Bobby said to Glenda, *You know, today could be my birthday.*

Or mine, she said.

And there's no way of knowing. He said this as if he were a hundred years old.

A few days later, on an abandoned hill-farm near Loving, Bobby found a peach tree and gathered a creel full. He took green ones too. When he got home he decided it was such a great moment, it had to be somebody's birthday.

Let's just say it's everybody's birthday, Beckie said.

They knew the birthday song and they sang it together, the smaller kids glowing.

The next time Ruby was there, Beckie asked her mother how old she, Beckie, was. Her mother looked at her.

You don't know how old you are? Ruby asked.

No'm, Beckie said.

Why not?

Looks like I can't keep track of it.

Well, neither can I. I've got too much to keep track of as is.

Glenda, listening, took it upon herself to figure out time. She asked Ruby a lot of questions until she had all the birthdays straight. She needed the current date, which Ruby named as somewhere around Sept. 11, 1947. That evening after Ruby had gone again and the children had eaten their hominy and their spoonfuls of jelly, Glenda tallied up the years.

Bobby was twelve, Glenda was ten, Phyl was eight, Richard was seven, Beckie was six, Jimmy was four, Bev was three, and Jeannie was two. *More or less,* Glenda said.

The churchlady came back, this time with biscuits wrapped in a cloth and cold fried chicken in a paper bag. She had another lady with her. The lady wanted to see the baby, who was sitting in Phyl's arms in the dirt by the fire and who wasn't such a baby anymore. Phyl brought her over. The second lady stared at the baby for a few minutes, then scanned the faces of the bigger children.

Hit's hard to tell, said the lady.

The hair's lighter, said Mrs. Auberry.

And the eyes are different.

Glenda stepped in front of Phyl, lifted Jean, and put her over her shoulder. She glared at the women.

The baby, said the lady. *That's your half-sister, ain't it?*

No, ma'am, that's our sister, said Glenda.

I heard that's the sheriff's baby, the woman said.

She's ourn.

Well, we wanted to come up here and see you'uns for ourselves since America died.

America?

Your grandmother.

She died?

Yes, a while back. You didn't know?

Mama didn't tell us.

After that nobody came for a very long time.

Chapter 28

Bobby

That's why I have to blame an entire community. A lot of people knew we were up there in the woods and those people could have done something. But they didn't. They didn't want to get involved. Maybe they didn't have enough for their own families to eat, so they just shoved us to the backs of their thoughts. I know when people like Mrs. Carolina Auberry saw Mama in town, she knew in the front of her mind where Mama's younguns were, up a mountain in an old shack, freezing to death or starving to death or hankering to death for a kind word or a soft, loving hand.

September 1947 would have been almost exactly two years since Mr. Allen and Ruby took us by mule and wagon up to that godforsaken place in Loving. Imagine little kids like us making it mostly by ourselves for two long years.

The time would double before we got out, before that harbor vanished in our rearview mirror.

Sometime around that September, on one of my rambles, I heard my mother referred to as a streetwoman. I didn't yet know what that word meant, although I had a general idea.

Chapter 29

Bobby learns more information about his mother.

It seemed like all Ruby had to do was look at Phyl and she'd get mad. It was worse after Red showed up then left again. When Phyl heard Ruby coming up the trail, if Phyl was lucky enough to hear rocks tumbling or a voice, she would run hide under the house before Ruby saw her. All of the children took to warning Phyl. Everybody was on high alert for Ruby.

One day, however, Ruby caught Phyl in the house. She sent everybody out.

After a while they heard Phyl screaming. She screamed for a minute then there was a slapping sound and Phyl was quiet.

When she came out she had blood running down her leg. She walked slowly toward the spring.

Phyl! Bobby said. *Are you okay?*

She didn't say anything.

Phyl! What happened?

Still she said nothing.

Bobby ran after her. *Phyl, say something. What happened?*

Phyl never said a word.

She stayed under the house the rest of the afternoon. Toward evening they heard a horn blowing somewhere in the valley. Ruby grabbed her things and quickly left.

The next day Bobby caught a ride to town and went straight to Anderson's Tourist Court. It was a long, low building made of red brick that sat close to the ground, underneath a mountain. It looked out on an arm of the lake. It had trees in the yard, shrubbery around the building and down the driveway, and a few beds with flowers blooming in them.

In the middle of the structure a sign said OFFICE. Bobby went inside. A teenage girl with blonde hair in ringlets past her shoulders, chewing gum, looked up. *May I help you?*

Bobby inquired as to Ruby Woods's room number. *She asked me to come,* he said. *She said she has some work.*

Nineteen, the girl said, uninterested. *That's around back.*

Bobby went back outside into the clairvoyant sunshine. He rounded a corner and passed Door No. 11, then Door No. 12. All the doors were brown. He kept going. Door No. 19 was dark-brown and shut. When he got to it he paused under a little awning over the door. He had not knocked and soon realized he was hearing voices inside, coming through an open window—his mother's voice, yes, and the voice of a man.

It is what it is, the man was saying.

But you said you'd think about a divorce, the woman said.

I've thought about it, he said. *Baby, I think about it every day. You know I'd lose my job and everything else.*

But we could be together.

We are together, he said. *What are we right now but together? Come here.*

We could go someplace else, she said.

You've got your kids to look after, anyway, he said. *We couldn't take all that on.*

There was a pause. *My kids,* she said sarcastically.

They are yours.

I didn't ask for them.

Ask for or not, they're up there.

Partly yours, she said.

One out of how many?

She didn't answer. After a minute she said, *You and I could start over. Like we were back in school and none of this other ever happened.*

Yeah, he said. *We sure used to cut the rug, didn't we? Remember that night after the dance? You were wearing that yellow dress.*

She laughed.

You got all the way to the top of the firetower in it. Woo-wee, he said. *I'll never forget that night.*

She laughed again, and the conversation trailed off, and other sounds began, and Bobby, feeling sick in his stomach, moved off.

The children presented Mr. Fiveash with a list of grocery items and he filled the order, except that Glenda had written "peppermint candy" on the list and Mr. Fiveash had scratched that off.

About a mile out of town a truck approached him from behind. He stuck out his thumb and the driver stopped. He never had to pull off the highway, traffic was so scant. The door was painted "Morganton Hardware" and the driver, a boy not much older than Bobby himself, motioned for him to get in the back. Bobby sat with the wind blowing hair into his eyes, watching the lake shrink into the distance, the mountains flow past, and then the creek unspool behind him. At the post office at Loving the truck paused long enough for the driver to hand a paper-wrapped parcel to Mrs. Hunt. Bobby jumped down and headed across the road.

Hey! the driver called. *That's a nickel.*

Bobby stopped. *I ain't got a nickel,* he said.

Then what'd you git on for?

You didn't say nothing about no nickel.

You didn't say you were bumming.

Bobby looked across at the chain of mountains to the north. The ridge was lined with the sticks of trees, leafless and naked, like an odd and branching fence. *Here's what I say*, Bobby called. *You can go to hell.* He turned and raced down Old Chapel Road toward Pleasant Gap Tarplay. Once he looked back and saw that, as he expected, the other boy had not left his truck. Still, he didn't feel good about what he'd done. He sure didn't need more enemies.

When he got to the church he found the door unlocked and he went inside and sat on the first bench, catching his breath and smelling the rich odor of white pine, sawn and polished. The windows had no panes, and the shutters were latched. Light leaked around the casements in rectangles. But the church was too dark, and the dimness made him uncomfortable. He remembered the new grave and he left by the front door, closing it behind him, and walked around the side of the church. He stopped once, as he had done many times, to kneel down and look under the old building. Its foundation was solid rock, just that, rocks dragged up from elsewhere to bear the weight of the old frame structure.

The graveyard was not fenced. The fresh grave made a mound of reddish dirt chocked with rocks. Already a marker had been hewn from a wooden slab, and a name had been freshly carved in it. *America M. Allen*, it said.

America Allen. He recognized with a shock that he was standing before his grandmother's grave. This was the closest he could remember being to her. She was no more than a few feet below him, lying dead in a pine box. He had seen it with his own eyes. He slowly knelt, his knees in the freshly turned black dirt. *Sept. 27, 1891-May 6, 1947,* the marker said. He put his hands on the hump of ground. This was his grandmother.

An urge hit him then, and strange as it was, he did not deny it. He slowly lay next to the grave, up so close to the mound of earth that he felt its length, its heft, its warmth, its bumps. He felt welcomed, wanted. The events of the day caught up with him then, and he fell asleep. When he woke, a sickle moon like a boat was visible in the western sky, darkness was almost upon him, and somewhere nearby a whippoorwill called. He set out quickly for home through blinking fireflies.

At home Glenda told him by firelight that Ruby was still gone. He knew that already. *Hawley the Horrible came and got her,* Glenda said. *That was his horn.*

Where's Phyl?

I can't get her out from under the house.

Bobby walked through the flickering light over to the porch and knelt to look underneath. He might as well have been gazing into a cavern or a cistern.

Phyl? he said.

There was no answer.

He traced in full darkness to the back of the house, where the house met the mountain. He thought he heard a shifting sound from beneath the house, and he bent again, as if speaking to the planks.

Phyl? It's okay, he said. *She's gone. Come on out now.*

I'm hurt, she said.

She hurt you? he said.

Phyl didn't respond.

Can you get out or you need help?

I can do it.

When Phyl crawled free of the house she stood slowly. Glenda had chunked sticks on the fire and it threw off light enough to see. Grimacing, Phyl limped to the fire. The children sat quietly, watching her. Glenda was dishing up hominy. Phyl's eyes looked like red pufferfish and one cheek flowered blue. Her red hair had snagged leaves and needles and all of it stuck out like a burning bush.

The children stared at her, then Glenda handed her a bowl and Bobby started talking again. He told them about the boy driving the hardware truck and how he, Bobby, had run. The children, already sleepy, ate with determination. Bobby told them that he'd found Mrs. Allen's grave.

So what Mrs. Auberry said was true, Glenda said.

I guess so, said Bobby. *Unless two go by that name.*

Who is Mrs. Allen? asked Beckie.

Mr. Allen's wife. Our grandmother.

I wonder how Mr. Allen is doing, said Glenda.

No way of knowing.

The entire time they sat around, doves mourned and bats came out, diving into the clearing. Far off a whippoorwill, perhaps the very one Bobby had heard mourning over his grandmother's grave, kept up its lonely, insistent call. Phyl did not speak.

In many ways she never spoke again.

Chapter 30

Bobby

Phyl told me years later what happened. I'll tell it just like it was told to me. I'm warning you, it's an awful story. Terrible. It's the worst kind of thing to know about and even worse to experience. But it's part of the story, like it or not. Phyl was raped by a broomstick. She was tied to the bed. Why? Because Phyl reminded Ruby of Red. Because Red did Ruby dirty and Ruby never got over it. Ruby wasn't without blame in that marriage by any means but Red misled her. He fell out of love with her. He cheated on her. He abandoned her. All that hatred she felt toward him she took out on Phyl. Also because the baby would *stop* crying when Phyl picked it up. But it would *keep on* crying when Mama picked it up. The baby thought of Phyl as her mama, and Ruby was jealous of that. She told Phyl that she'd make sure she never had young'uns. And she did.

Chapter 31

Bobby decides that it's time to act.

I'm going hunting, Bobby said to Glenda that morning.

Try to get back before dark, she said. *It's scarier when you're not here.*

I know.

I hope you find bread, she said. *But we'll take anything.*

He hiked to the highway fast and without pause, then turned down the mountain toward Morganton. A car passed and he waved with both arms. It was a black Ford that pulled off the road a few hundred feet ahead. He ran toward it, hand gripped around the neck of his sack. Inside the Ford a middle-aged man sported a white shirt with a tie and a black fedora.

Hop in, son, the man said.

The boy glanced toward the back seat and hesitated.

Up here is fine, the man said. Round, gold-rimmed glasses softened his eyes.

The boy got in and set his sack by his feet.

Where you headed?

Morganton, sir.

Well, it's a pretty day for a trip to town, the man said. *What you got ahead of you?*

Not much, said Bobby. He eased his foot sideways to touch the rock.

I did a lot of that when I was a boy, the man said. He wore a dark suit and had a gold band on his marriage finger. *Rambling. What's your name?*

Bobby, the boy said.

That doesn't tell me much, the man said. He spoke kindly, even smiled.

Woods, the boy said.

Are you Grover's boy?

Nosir, Bobby said. He didn't mention the uncle part.

Who are your folks?

I don't have many folks, the boy said.

They rode in silence for as much as a mile or two, the creek now along to the left, the man driving slowly and carefully. He took up whistling after a minute, a tune Bobby couldn't identify.

I've been up close to the line, the man said suddenly, pensively. *A case up there.*

Bobby was silent.

It's looking like a man poisoned his wife. And I have to represent him. He glanced quickly at Bobby. *I'm an attorney,* the man said. *District attorney. You know what that is?*

Yessir. But he didn't.

Vandieviere, the man said. *Henry Grady Vandieviere.*

Yessir, Bobby said. *Thank you for stopping.*

They were passing the Loving Post Office. The postmistress was watering some begonias set out in coffee cans. Mr. Vandieviere honked his horn as they approached, then stuck out his arm.

Mrs. Susie Hunt, he said. *She's been there since I was a boy.*

They passed Loving School. The children were outside at recess, thirty or forty of them standing in groups or dashing about the schoolyard.

Why aren't you in school, son?

I don't know, sir, said Bobby.

The man looked at him again. *You don't know?*

Nosir. My mama doesn't send me.

You okay, son?

Yessir.

You look like a man with a load on your mind.

Not much, sir.

Well then.

They rode on and the man took up his whistling again, same tune. As they crossed the big creek near the Baptist Church, Vandieviere asked where he wanted to get out.

Anywhere'll do.

Vandieviere drove to the courthouse and parked. On the courthouse lawn two men in workboots studied a dead tree. One of them held a crosscut saw in his hands.

You know that tree?

The one dead there?

That one. The man was gathering up a leather satchel.

You mean what type it is?

Yes, the species.

Nosir.

It's a chestnut. That was a beautiful tree. A blight is taking them out. I thought that one would survive, up here in town, but the blight got it too. A shame.

Yessir.

The boy climbed out and closed the door behind him.

Well, stay out of trouble, the man said.

Yessir. I will.

Bobby gripped his sack. He remembered something and turned back.

Thank you for the ride, sir.

Not a worry, the man said. *Hold a minute, son.* He fished in his pocket and found something, pulled it out and held his hand toward Bobby. Between his thumb and forefinger was a coin.

Buy yourself a candy bar.

Yessir, the boy said. *Thank you, sir.*

The boy started off down the wooden sidewalk. The sun was high in the sky, almost overhead, and the day was heating up. He felt the coin in his palm and he thought about Mr. Vandieviere. The coin gave him something palpable. It was a power. He felt it distinctly. A coin was power. It was his. One day he hoped to be able to hand a kid a coin. But that was far off, way out in some other galaxy, and he doubted luck would get him there, to be the kind of man that could adjust his gold-rimmed glasses, reach into his suit pocket, and hand a kid a dime. Bobby could not conjure himself as that kind of man, since luck had never been on his side. Getting to be the kind of person who could give another a coin was going to take more than luck.

The town was humming, folks moving about in ones and twos, in and out of the drug store and the bank and the post office. Cars were parked along the street. A few mules were tied, and Bobby could hear mules heehawing down at Wishon Livery. A horse whinnied. It was spring and up in the trees birds were flying about and singing. Across the way a woman called to another, *We've got it already.*

When he was out of sight of the courthouse, Bobby felt the coin, now in his pocket. It was a dime. He felt a pang of hunger in his belly but that was nothing new. He kept walking, headed toward Anderson's Tourist Court. He could almost buy everybody a candy bar with a dime.

Chapter 32

Bobby

When a boy goes hunting with his father and bags his first deer, his father will smear some of the blood on his son's forehead. It's an initiation rite. Then his father will teach the son how to dress out an animal.

I learned to hunt with a slingshot. I got pretty good at it. I could take out a squirrel or a bird. We ate whatever I could kill. I was always looking for the perfect bullet for my slingshot. I liked them small and very round. Those kind were deadly.

I got good at slingshotting because of a rooster. Somebody's rooster got loose in the woods. We kids chased that rooster all over the mountain for at least a month. Every time the rooster got close, I practiced my aim. Hitting the body was no good. The feathers were like armor.

One day I got him right in the head. As you imagine, that rooster went in the pot.

After I got grown, I never touched a slingshot again. A slingshot is a deadly weapon. Any kind of rock will kill if it hits the right spot.

That day Mr. Vandieviere gave me a ride to town, I should have talked to him. God sent him to me. I had the chance right then to take the high road out of the mess my family was in.

But I couldn't talk.

Most of my life I had that problem. But I don't have it any more.

Chapter 33

The boy wants to destroy whatever stands in the way of love.

The hotel looked like a hospital with its red bricks and galvanized roof, although a narrow concrete porch ran the entire length. Small panes of glass, top to bottom, were set in the door to the office, and through it Bobby could see a lamp turned on. He noted again that all the room doors were chocolate brown. Outside each door was a concrete planter painted blue, filled with blood-red geraniums.

For a long time Bobby sat behind a tulip poplar and watched the room he knew belonged to his mother. It was quiet, no movement. He got up once or twice and went to a spigot and drank. An old, thin man in faded and patched overalls came back from his dinner and set to weeding a lengthy bed of daylilies that had not yet begun to bloom. After a while the old gardener found some business near the poplar.

You looking for somebody? he said.

My mother lives here, said Bobby.

Miss Ruby?

Yessir, Bobby said.

I don't believe she's here. She's usually at work this time of day.

I'll wait.

You Ruby's boy? the man asked.

Yessir, Bobby said.

Ummh, humh. The old man shook his head side to side as he grunted, the second sound lower in pitch than the first. That's all he said.

The afternoon crested and waned. At some point Bobby fell asleep and when he woke, dark had fallen. He jerked his head up and looked around with a strange concern in his eyes as he forced them to adjust to the wild darkness. Something had wakened him and he was glad it had. How could he have fallen asleep? He could have lost his opportunity. And now Glenda was alone in the dark with the kids.

He heard footsteps on gravel behind him. He stayed crouched behind a hedge of mountain laurel. Lights were on in his mother's room, the curtain opened a few inches. A muscular man in uniform went to Ruby's door and knocked lightly. She let him in. The curtain closed.

Bobby opened his sack and took out the rock. It was a useful rock, not too heavy, perfectly shaped, coming to a point. He had looked a long time for this rock, and when he spotted it, he knew immediately it was the right one.

He waited a few minutes. A man and a woman exited a room a few doors down and walked off toward town, the woman's heels clicking on the sidewalk. Bobby quickly crossed the lawn to the brown door and slowly turned the knob. There was a pause in the sounds from inside.

What was that? his mother said.

Bobby waited.

Probably one of those cats.

The door was locked. Bobby knocked on it, kind of lightly.

I knew I heard something, Ruby said. *Who is it?* (This louder.)

Bobby did not answer, knocked again.

After some scrambling the door opened and his mother, holding a yellow housecoat closed, stood silhouetted against the globed light. Bobby burst in the door, knocking Ruby backwards. She fell against a table there and that's when Bobby delivered his first blow, catching her against the head with the dull end of the stone. She went down.

What the hell? Hawley said. Bedsprings creaked violently. The man was completely naked but he was going for his belt, where his gun was holstered. Bobby leapt for him. He swung his rock at the side of the man's head but the man ducked instinctively, then punched Bobby as hard as he could in the gut. Bobby straightened up and came at the man again. He managed to pound some blows onto his shoulders and neck until the man punched him again, even harder, in the right eye. For a minute Bobby's eye lit like fireworks, and the pain bloomed like a poppy through his head. He couldn't see. He still had the rock but he was staggering, trying to get his bearings in the unfamiliar room.

He was hearing movement all around him, in front and behind. Another blow to the jaw sent him reeling to the floor. The floor came at him too fast, and he felt the pain of it in his hip and shoulder as he hit the cold wood, face to the side. He scrambled to get to his feet but no part of him functioned properly.

Then he heard the distinct click of a hammer drawn back. He waited for the shot.

The woman was screaming. Now someone outside was pounding on the door.

Ruby. The man was panting. *Hand me the gun.*

Bobby opened his one good eye. His mother's housecoat had come open and she was fully naked beneath. She was holding a revolver pointed at his heart. She saw that he had seen her, that he was looking at her, still slim and beautiful, her hips wide, her legs pretty, her breasts large and full. She had a wild look in her eyes. She raised the revolver and aimed it at his face.

No, Ruby, the man said. *Did you hear me? Hand. Me. The. Gun.*

Hawley moved sideways, careful, and took the gun from the woman.

Isn't that ... the man trailed off.

It's Bobby, the woman said. She drew her housecoat tight and tied it.

Chapter 34

Bobby

I slept in a hedge that night after Hawley kicked me out of the room, and I mean literally kicked me, and the next day I limped back out to the road and caught a ride in a mule wagon with a weedy farmer in faded overalls and a heavyset girl that might have been his daughter or might have been his wife.

At Fiveash's store I limped inside and bought all the candy a dime would buy, licorice and butterscotch and bubblegum.

After that Ruby didn't come for four months. That was the longest time, I think. By then I was old enough to keep up with a calendar and so was Glenda. I stayed out of town for a long time. Then anger took hold of me again and I stopped caring. I saw Ruby sometimes, when I sneaked into Morganton and watched Anderson's from the trees. I was careful—very careful—not to get caught. Sometimes I saw her coming and going. I saw the sheriff too. After a while I went wherever I wanted to go.

When Christmas came around again, our Daddy came for a visit, all the way from Michigan. He must have found Ruby in town, because somebody told him where the cabin was and one cold day he came climbing up the trail. You never saw a person more shocked than I was to see my own pa coming through the bushes. I thought we were rescued for sure. He had some presents for us down in the car, and we all went down to where he'd parked outside Fiveash's, and he pulled out the gifts. What he brought was junk, nothing more than junk, plastic balls about the size of oranges, plastic barrettes for the girls, a pack of pencils. What in the world were we going to do with pencils? He didn't know his own kids, but we told him all our names and how old we were. The little kids were afraid of him. Phyl hung back too, but by then she was afraid of everybody.

I asked him if we could come live with him, and Glenda begged him the same, but he couldn't be moved. He told us he had a new wife and that we had some brothers and sisters we'd never met. It turns out that some of our siblings were about the same age we were.

When he left we knew for a fact that we wouldn't be able to count on Red. That knowledge rode hard in us and set us back spiritually, if you know what I mean. I'd say, knowing what I know now about life, that we were lost in a wilderness.

We did get down out of that holler where we were put to die. It took another year or so but we got out. It wasn't the way we wanted to get out, but looking back, I believe it was for the best. What came afterward wasn't easy on any of us. But compared to what we had, it was the best thing.

The end came about because of a moonshine still. This was still in the days of Prohibition.

Chapter 35

An active moonshine still is the beginning of the end.

Later that same spring Glenda went with Bobby to look for the patch of ramps he had located. Every year since that first time they had hunted them up again. Now they were charging groceries on a regular basis with Fiveash but they never turned down an opportunity to supplement the dry beans and white rice. Glenda and Bobby too had become decent cooks, and even Richard and Beckie were learning their way around a fire.

On the day they went ramp-hunting, Glenda and Bobby left all the kids at home because it was a long walk and they needed their hands free. Alone they could go faster and tote more. Phyl and Richard would watch the younger ones.

Bobby remembered pretty well how to get to the ramp cove. They could climb straight up then cut across the ridge to the next holler and go down it a ways. That would be the safest way. By now they had a trail from the cabin up to the ridge, or at least if a person was paying attention they could tell it was a trail.

As they angled off the ridge Glenda told Bobby to stop and be quiet. *I hear something,* she said.

What is it?

Like voices. Listen.

Bobby couldn't hear anything that sounded like voices. He heard wind in the ridge trees. He heard a high whistle that he knew to be a hawk.

They went on, leaves rasping under their feet, and limbs of hemlock and fir making brushing sounds as they passed. Glenda was carrying a pillowcase and Bobby hauled a sheet.

Stop. Be quiet, Glenda said.

Bobby thought he could hear water coming out of the mountain making a little seep, toward where they were headed. Ramps grew in that damp area and he could already smell the wild onion.

It's people, she said.

Who'd be up in here? he asked. *You know the answer to that. Just us. Nobody else.* But right then he heard something metal bang, then all was deathly quiet for a while.

He looked at Glenda. *It* is *people. What are they doing?*

Her eyes were round and blue as morning glories. *I don't know.*

We better go see. They might be coming for us.

As the children proceeded they heard more noises, kind of spooky, like people trying to be quiet but too involved in something to manage it. They got almost down to the creek. After a while they stuck their makeshift sacks under a bush and crept forward across a slice of granite. Bobby had been to that place lots of times. It was a wet mineral plateau that looked down on clear water running through large slabs of granite. The granite was flecked with mica and quartz. Its underside stayed constantly dampened by the water thrown up from the creek, he knew, and there green moss softened the rock. He and Glenda crouched and slid across the bald boulder, then took a look over the ledge.

Five or six men had a fire going. A kettle perched tilted on the fire and some kind of contraption was set up near the creek. Full bags of something leaned against a white pine. *Corn,* Bobby thought.

Just then one of the fellows at the kettle looked up. He dropped a ladle in his hands and in the same motion pulled a revolver from his belt. In a split second every other man did the same until a posse of guns were pointing at Bobby and Glenda.

Bobby stood up then, on the boulder, not wanting a misunderstanding. He wasn't dumb. He knew what they had come across. He opened his arms out wide, baring his skinny chest, until he stood in the shape of a crucifix. *We're no harm to you*, he called. *Just my sister and me. We just come through hunting ramps.*

Three of the men had already begun their ascent of the boulder, leaping up the mica-flecked granite. Glenda rose to her feet.

The first fellow had a bald head and beady black eyes. His eyes were cold. *Whatcha doin here?*

We're no harm, Bobby said again, his arms still open. *It's just my sister and me. We come through hunting ramps.*

Where you live?

Down yonder.

Down yonder where.

The cabin up from Fiveash's Store.

I've never seen a cabin beyond Fiveash's.

Yessir, there's one. And we live there.

Who's we?

Our folks, said Bobby.

A second and a third man were obviously twins, both tall and thin, with lank, greasy hair hanging down around their necks. One was an exact replica of the other. They were staring at Glenda. She was studying the ground.

You-uns up here, we don't care, said Bobby. *We didn't mean to disturb you. We just heard talking and we're not used to people talking up in here, so we came to see who it was. We don't mean nothing. We'll let you get back to what you were doing.*

And you'll never mention it to nobody, said a fourth man, not more than twenty and wormy-looking, pale-faced.

Nosir, not to anybody, Bobby said.

You talk, we'll find you, said the kid.

'Thout a doubt, the bald man echoed. He looked entirely capable of all manner of wrongdoing.

We got no problem finding you. An older, pokier man who looked like a prototype of the two tall fellows had been listening from the rock. He chuckled. *Yeah, we got no problem finding you.*

We won't talk, Bobby said. *Like I say, we live up on the mountain and we don't see nobody nohow. We're sure sorry we bothered you. We'll head on about our business.*

Not so fast, said one of the twins. *Who's this pretty girl with you?* The man took a step toward Glenda, his brother shadowing him.

Just my sister, said Bobby.

What's yore name, pretty girl? The man rubbed his hand on his buttock as if to brush off dust and dirt, then reached out and touched Glenda's wavy, dark hair. He put his nasty fingers deep in her curls and then brought them down past her neck, to her chest.

His brother said, *Wait, little brother. This is mine too.*

Bobby stepped between the man and Glenda. He became a different person then and everyone on the boulder felt it and knew it and understood it. They knew intimately what it was like to be a person who shapeshifted, who was one person most of the time but who shifted into another, into being a person to be reckoned with. *Don't touch her,* Bobby said quietly. Later he lamented having no weapon—no knife, no gun, no rock, nothing.

Ain't worth it, said the old man. *Step back, boys. We got work waiting on us.*

You got work I could do? asked Bobby.

This is man's work, said the old guy.

I can do it, sir.

We can't use you. You-uns go on home. Don't come back this way, unless you want us to deliver on the little promise we made you.

Yessir.

Bobby headed out, Glenda shadowing him. They grabbed their sack and blanket and headed back up toward the ridge, walking fast. When they got into the trees good, Bobby picked up the pace until he was running. He could hear Glenda running behind. In a few minutes he stopped and she stopped. They looked behind them. The woods were empty, except for the white pines that limned the bare rocks with their sienna colored needles.

They were winded when they got to the ridge. Bobby turned west toward the cove, walking again. About then he heard a little noise from Glenda and he stepped to the side so she wouldn't run into him from behind and he looked at her.

Her cheeks were blood-red and wet. Her eyes were big and bloodshot and wet.

You okay, Bobby said. *Ain't no need to cry.* They were stopped at a place on the mountain that opened up into a lot of rock. The rock had little pockets and holes where rainwater collected.

Maybe that's where Bobby learned that it's useless to tell somebody not to cry. When he said it, Glenda started crying harder, but quietly. She bent her head and put her face in her hands. Her fingernails were down to the quick and dirty all around them, and suddenly Bobby saw that his sister could be pretty if she had half a chance. She stood there in the mountain air with her face in her hands, an empty yellowed pillowcase under one arm. Her whole body trembled, shaking like the last beech leaf on a tree in winter, when the wind catches it.

Glenda said something that came out muffled.

I can't understand you, Bobby said.

She lifted her face. It was a terrible sight. *They're gonna come after me*, she said.

They're not coming, Bobby said. *They don't know where we live.*

They'll find us, she said. *Me.*

Bobby looked down at the gray rock. One of the holes was perfectly round. They'd seen it a lot of times. They'd put their hands down in it to feel its smooth and perfect sides. Richard thought it was where Cherokee women had ground their corn, but Bobby wasn't sure. He knew that a rock could get caught in a little hole and grind it out over time, even into a perfect circle.

He could hear a little trickle of water coming right out of the mountainside and heading on down through a boggy area, and he could hear Glenda hiccupping.

Hush, now, he said. *I'm never gonna let them hurt you. We're gonna be okay.*

We're never gonna be okay, she said, and in his heart Bobby knew, of course, that she was right.

Chapter 36

Bobby

That our mother didn't want us was obvious. Her people didn't want us. I've had to accept that my dad didn't either. He let all that happen to us. He knew we were up the mountain. When he came to visit us that one time, if he had cared, he could have brought us down, taken care of us like a man's supposed to take care of his flesh and blood.

He just turned around and went back to Michigan, back to his other family.

There's not a human being on this earth wanted a daddy more than I did. And a mother. And a home. Not having one was an unbearable serving of pain that I could not tolerate. Some part of me even then knew I would never have it. It would be a thing guaranteed to most kids but something I would never know, although after my own kids were born, I got to be on the other end of the level, and I knew how to do the job even though it wasn't done for me.

I've tried to come to terms with that.

There are some things that happen to a kid that can never be fixed. Everywhere that kid goes, all the way through adulthood, through all the places they're going to live and all the things they manage to do, the hard times stay inside them. Sometimes the bad stuff shrivels up into little balls as hard as hickory nuts, but it never goes away. People think kids are resilient but they're not. Kids are the most fragile beings on the planet.

Chapter 37

One of the moonshiners conducts surveillance.

One day that spring, the third year, foraging for twigs and limbs, Richard noticed brown splotches on a bare rock. From that vantage the shanty could be seen through the spare branches of trees.

What do you think this is? he asked.

Bird poop, said Glenda.

Richard bent down. *What I thought,* he said.

What?

Smell it, he said.

Glenda bent down and sniffed. *Snuff.*

I wish we had a dog, Jimmy said.

Me too, said Glenda.

As spring progressed, the children found more evidence of a snuff-dipper who came at intervals to watch them. Then one afternoon an affable man in black trousers ambled up the path from the road. He wore black glasses. He introduced himself as Preacher Culpepper. He asked the kids a lot of questions, which they answered as best they could.

How'd you know we were up here? Glenda asked him.

He said a man had seen them and had come by his church, First Baptist of Morganton, and told him. The man had said something needed to be done.

The preacher told the man that he'd come and check on the situation.

Sometime later Preacher Culpepper returned with a box of food. Not long after that he came with a sack of used clothes. On that visit he asked the children if they wanted to stay up there like they were living. They said they did. Even so, Bobby could feel a change coming at him and he wanted to stop it, to slow it down long enough to let him think, to make a plan, to formulate a future for them in which he could stay in control and take care of everybody, get them grown. He had felt this before, as far back as Michigan, before he ever knew they were leaving, which they had done, one gray morning on a choo-choo train. He had wanted to put his heels down to slow everything, so that he could think. Even then he knew he would fail.

Chapter 38

Bobby

I remember when we'd get up we'd walk through the woods. I can still remember a place where we'd look across at a mountainside and see what looked like a tulip field, with a million wildflowers.

I thought it was something I dreamed.

We ate whatever we could find in the mountains. I think back on the things we ate—it was wild apples, pears, black walnuts, hickory nuts, poke salat, berries, black grapes. A lot of times there was no food.

We were a part of that mountain and a part of the woods.

It wasn't a dream.

Chapter 39

When it comes, the rescue (if you want to call it that) is swift and sudden.

The day started out like any other day, except Glenda cried. She had been crying more often. When Beckie got a splinter Glenda cried. When she tore her dress she cried. She cried when she had to make another kettle of hominy. When Beckie mentioned that Glenda was growing breasts like Ruby, Glenda cried. *Shut up*, she said. She cried when Bobby brought home a sack of figs. The day Fiveash told Bobby that he couldn't charge any more she cried on and off all day.

Did you ask him why? she said.

Mr. Allen told him it was over.

Mr. Allen's got money, she said. *He's got food. He's got a good house. And he's our grandfather. It's not like we're somebody else's grandyounguns.*

Yeah.

What's going to happen to us? she wailed.

Stop crying, Bobby said. *You cry too much.*

That was not the right thing to say. Glenda fell to the straw tick, sobbing inconsolably. When Glenda cried, Bobby had a feeling that the container of their lives had rusted out, with holes in the bottom, and whatever they were was leaking out and disappearing into the ground.

Later, Bobby would remember every small detail of the morning. Lying alone in his dormitory bunk, he would live it over and over. Fall had come again. Glenda had slow-boiled some of the Fiveash apples into sauce, and she had managed to make hoecakes on the fire. The bottoms burned but the children didn't care. Bobby had taken charge more as he grew older, and now he told everybody while they were eating that they had to get in all the firewood possible, that it was time, and to stack it under the edge of the porch. All that space had to be filled, he said. He had to go hunting, to make a walkabout for food. He figured privately that he could pay a visit to the Grover's smokehouse. Beckie said she had to do the wash. She said Little Beckie's dress got dirty playing around the fire, but it wouldn't take long.

The morning was young when it became apparent that a number of folks were approaching. They heard a man's voice. Phyl headed for the house, Glenda close behind.

I hear a woman too, Bobby said.

Glenda stopped. *I wonder if it's Mama*, she said.

Mama's coming, Mama's coming, sang Beckie.

They kept listening. Richard, like a kid will do, walked out the path made over time, out to the trail. Phyl had set down Jeannie and backed up until her scrawny backbone was touching the porch. She eased along the porch to the back corner and intently watched the path.

Three people entered the clearing—a man in a white cotton, long-sleeved shirt with a jacket over it, a short-haired woman in blousy dark-blue britches, and Preacher Culpepper wearing a pair of nice overalls and a straw hat. *Hello, son,* the preacher said to Richard, who stood watching, speechless. None of the other visitors said anything. They had paused to look around.

They saw a falling-down cabin. They saw a skinny girl in ragged clothes pressed against the far side of a rotting porch. They saw a patch of bare ground with some rocks dragged up around a fire. They saw Glenda and a couple of kids of toddling size and Jimmy with his legs stuck far out of his overall legs.

The woman in the strange pants glanced at the white-shirted man, and her pinkish mouth formed itself into a thin line. Then the folks walked up to the fire. They asked a lot of questions—if their mother was home and where she might be, had she been there the night before, when was the last time she'd been there, what they had to eat in the house, did they have anything for breakfast, when was the last time they'd been in school.

After a while the man in the suit coat asked Mrs. Peabody to step off a ways, and they conversed in low tones. When they stepped back the man explained that the kids couldn't stay where they were. It wasn't safe, he said, for children to be scrabbling for a living up in a holler by themselves. He said that someone had reported them. *I am taking you to a good home,* he said.

Nosir, Jimmy said to him. *We have to stay here. We have a mama. Ruby is going to come back and we need to be here when she gets home. So she won't be worried about us.*

The man and woman exchanged glances. Preacher Culpepper adjusted his glasses.

We'll let her know where you are, he said.

We want to stay here, Richard said.

Well, let's go find your mother, the man said.

The days ahead of them would become a blurry cloud that floated in on a mountain-storm and left everything shrouded in fog and mist. There would be their mother screaming at the folks. There would be their grandfather watching from the edge of a circle, the emotions on his face unreadable. There would be Ruby pounding on the car, Glenda crying, and Beckie crying, and Richard crying. There would be a hospital in Hapeville, which sounded like Hateville, where a doctor would look for things wrong with them. There would be temporary placement in Bartow Children's Home.

Orphanage, Glenda would whisper to Bobby.

The first day they were at Hateville their Mama was there. The folks were trying to get all the paperwork straight. Most of the children didn't have a birth certificate. When a woman with a clipboard asked Ruby when Glenda was born, she said 1937. She said Nov. 29. She said the girl's full name was Glenda Beatrice. Beckie was Rebecca Elaine and she was born Nov. 28, Phyllis Loretta was born Nov. 11, and Richard Wesley was born Nov. 14. Four of them were born in November.

Bobby was born May 14, 1935, and Robert was the only name he ever knew he had. Jimmy was James Donald.

All that first day at Hateville disappeared in a confounding haze.

The children would be separated, girls in one direction and boys in another. There would be Phyl looking back, not letting go of Norma Jean's and Beverly Ann's hands. There would be a stack of clean used clothing handed to Bobby, along with a towel, a washcloth, and soap. There would be lice treatments and meals served on plates, with forks, knives, and spoons, glasses of milk. The plates would be piled with warm and delicious food. There would be eight children eating as if they had been starved.

For Bobby, there would be the urge to run, to make a break, to try to make it on his own at fourteen. Every time he would make up his mind to run, he'd think about Richard and Jimmy, *Is this our new house? Do we get a new mama too? Do we get a daddy?*

That was all ahead of them. *The car's down at the store*, the man was saying. *You can't stay here. Best douse that fire. Get whatever you want to bring. You won't be coming back this way.*

When the children were taken, all they had was on their backs and in one small sack. Just like that, the shaky civilization they had built with such innocence and such determination crumbled into ruins.

Chapter 40

Bobby

The full name of the place we ended up was the Georgia Baptist Children's Home. It was far from the mountains, down in the flatlands. They had to drive us five or six hours to get there. Every mile was a brick on my chest until I could barely take a breath. I should have been like Glenda, sobbing. I couldn't cry or process that realm of emotion. What I did was get angry.

I knew I'd never see my mother again. How would she find us six hours away from Morganton? How would she get to us? The closest town was Baxley, and that was almost twelve or fifteen miles away. Surely a bus ran to Baxley, but how would Mama get on down to us?

People called it "The Home." For us, it was *a* home, but not *home*. It was not the loving home I craved. In fact, I hated the children's home with a passion. We had a house mother and a house father, but not a real mother or a real father.

The girls went to a girls' house and we boys went to a boys' house, so our family got separated. On Sundays in church and other times when the whole orphanage assembled, I got to see Phyl and Beckie and all the rest. I never talked to them about the past. I barely talked to them at all. In that new place I tried not to think of the old place. I tried to just figure my way into a new life and make the best out of the new place, which was a lot of church-going and a lot of schooling and a lot of fussing.

We had to adjust. They served sweet tea with every meal, for example, caramel stuff in a glass with ice. We'd never had tea. Truthfully, I was scared to drink it at first. I had no clue what it was, and I figured it was poison. But we had to eat all the food on our plates before we left the table. I got used to it.

Mostly there was a lot of working. The Home was really a big farm. It had gardens where we all helped grow sweet corn, field peas, and tomatoes. It had fields of tobacco, and the bigger kids had to crop tobacco all summer during the hottest summers you ever saw. The Home had a dairy, which is where I worked. There's a lot to a dairy. After school and on Saturdays I had to work like a full-grown man, driving cows in and out of the barn, cleaning their udders, hooking up the milking machines. I had to haul hay with an old Farmall tractor, and I had to fork manure out of the holding pens. In the spring there's all the weanlings to contend with. They holler for their mamas and their mamas holler for them. It's enough to drive a man crazy, all that hollering. We would pour milk by the gallon into buckets with nipples, and the calves learned to drink from them. After a few weeks they'd stop pining so bad for their mamas. When I was older I had to get up at 3:30 in the morning to milk before school.

I never did adjust to flat country. My feet always felt like they should be either going up or down. Flat country makes you lazy, except we didn't have time to be lazy.

I ran away from the children's home at least a dozen times. I don't know why I ran away so much. I guess I was looking for something. One time I hitchhiked to Baxley. Someone called the home and Mr. Berry, who was in charge of the farm operation, came and got me. Another time I got Phyl to run away with me. We decided we were going to Florida to pick oranges. *If you hold your dress up*, I said to her, *the big trucks will stop*. I have no idea how I knew that. We got to Alma, then on to Waycross, and then a mile from the Florida line. I don't know why, but we turned around and started hitchhiking back. I guess we got scared when we faced Florida for real. The state patrol picked us up in Waycross.

If I knew then what I knew now, I think I would have settled down and tried to weather childhood better than I did.

I've seen the paperwork. As a kid I couldn't have known this, but the paperwork says we were up on the mountain four years. That's what they figured. That means the baby was four years old when we got out. I was fourteen. Glenda was almost thirteen, Phyl was ten. And so on.

I still don't know how we did it. How we lived. How we survived.

This is what the papers from the Department of Public Welfare said: "These children lived in a shanty high on the side of a mountain, which to reach one must walk a mile and a half after he drives as far as he can, the only road to the place being a foot path through briars and bushes. In reaching the shanty the Manager found his way through many briars and brambles with considerable scratches. The yard was grown up, the shanty falling to decay."

The paper keeps on going, describing things I remember there myself. "One jar of blackberries and some cold bread constituted the total food supply in the house."

Then it says, "The courts declared the home non-existent."

They were wrong about that. It existed. It may not have been a good home or an adequate home. I may not have had a father or a mother. I may not have had enough food. But I had a home. Yes, my brothers and sisters and I, we had a home.

When we got saved, they made sure we had clothes and food and a sound roof over our heads. We went to a Home. But what we never got was love.

Mama came to see us one time. I was in the ninth grade. That was the only time we ever saw her. Later, after we were grown, one of my brothers questioned her. *Why didn't you come any more?* Jimmy asked her. He was grown and working in Baxley by then.

They wouldn't let me, she said.

I know for a fact, he said, *that the children's home can not keep a parent from visiting.*

Ruby explained to Jimmy that her visit that one time affected us so badly that Mr. Creamer, the superintendent of the children's home, thought it would be better for her not to come back.

That made sense. It did. I guess.

Dad visited us once too, when I was in eleventh grade. That was the only time we saw him. He was still living in Trenton. He went on to have eight or nine kids besides us.

Our grandfather never came. Not one of our aunts or uncles came, none of our cousins. None of the community ever came to see us at Georgia Baptist Children's Home. Nobody ever wrote, ever called, ever questioned what happened. Nobody. Any of these necessarily wouldn't mean love, per se, but a visit would have gone a long way toward us *thinking* we were loved.

That's sad to me now, when I consider that the one thing I wanted above all else I could not have. I have been affected by all of it. Now it's hard to open up. I don't hardly talk about any of this at all.

I told you that if I was going to write a book, it would be for two reasons. One, I wanted to expose what happened. I've done that now. Two, I want folks to know that we survived.

I can't say that we didn't suffer. I guess I'm saying that nobody ended up in prison. I don't think any of us ever got addicted to alcohol or drugs. Most of us didn't smoke. Everybody held jobs and had families and lived productive lives and made good.

Some of us kept a lot of secrets. My brother told me that all his life he was consumed with guilt, that he hadn't done more or that he had done too much. He was always disturbed by the past, and I think that's one reason he got sick with his heart and died too young.

Here's what happened: I've already said that one of my brothers got a degree from the University of Florida and became an architect. He was mentally tough. He was a high diver, won all kinds of gold medals. Even though he's dead now, he still holds the world record, I hear, in his age category for cliff diving somewhere down in Panama.

When I got close to turning eighteen, I had a friend who had already aged out and gone down to Orlando to work construction, and I wrote him. He said I could come down. I got grown and the home gave me twenty dollars and a bus ticket.

Then Phyl turned eighteen and she joined me for a while, until she met her first husband. He turned out violent so she got away from him as soon as she could. After a while Phyl got a job running the bakery of a big supermarket. She worked there all her life and got a good retirement. She married again but that didn't work out either. She lived alone most of her life. She never did have children. Mama had made sure of that.

Glenda told me that after she left the orphanage, she made up a story about where she came from. She didn't tell anybody the truth, not even her husband and children. She didn't want to be dragged down by the past. And she wasn't. *I blocked it from my mind*, she said. *I didn't want anybody feeling sorry for me.* Finally when all the children got together in the eighties she decided to tell her husband. Now her children know, as well.

Richard became a contractor in Alabama. His number-one mission in life was to love his wife and children and to create the kind of home that all of them enjoyed being part of. But he never liked to be inside. He'd go into his house to eat supper, say, and then he'd go back outside. He'd work in his garden or trim trees or pick up limbs. Sometimes he'd sit in his Adirondack chairs, listen to the birds, and watch the clouds in the sky. He'd make phone calls sitting out there. Basically he ran his whole business and life from his yard.

Beckie married a handsome guy she met in high school. They stayed in south Georgia and created a prosperous business and a beautiful home. They had children and then grandchildren. She didn't dwell on the past.

Basically my story is the same. I had my first family and that broke up, and years later, I felt blessed to have a second chance with my second wife. I looked as if I were doing well with a nice house, nice furniture, nice vehicle, a nice yard; but I guess I was haunted. That's why I'm telling the story. I'm hoping to get out from under some of the burden of it.

I never did go back to the cabin. Jimmy went back up there one time. He told me that the cabin had fallen in, and the place was more growed-up than ever. He said that when he got up to it, it felt like a gunblast in his stomach, and of course him seeing it was enough for me.

Only three of us eight are left, and we're getting older every day. I'm glad our story is now told.

I should also tell you that I'm back in the mountains. Finally I have found again the place that saved me when I was a child, where I left boyhood and became a man, the mountains with their galax and laurel and bloodroots, mountain streams, hollers, old apple trees, a family in a wagon behind a horse, foxfire mountains which for these thirty years have been disappearing, cut open by roads and bleeding to death, dried up by a sun growing hotter. Finally I am back in a loving place I knew existed but which I could not approach.

The rest of it, it's all in my heart. It sits here, little and hard like a walnut, right in here. I don't reckon it will ever go away.

the end

ACKNOWLEDGMENTS

Thanks to you, dear reader, for giving this book a chance. Many thanks to the entire Woods family for sharing their story, assisting with research, and providing documents and memorabilia. I am especially indebted to the late Jimmy Woods, the late Phyllis Woods, and Richard Woods. Thanks to my late father, Franklin Ray, and my mother, Lee Ada Ray, for introducing me to them.

Thanks to my husband, Raven Waters, son Silas, daughter Skye, and all my friends and family.

A REQUEST

If you are moved to do so, please share this book with friends, family, and neighbors or recommend it to others. You may want to ask your librarian to obtain a copy for your local library. Telling friends about meaningful books is still the best way to allow a story to do its job, which is to touch us, open our hearts, and make us think.

In addition, reading a book in tandem with friends or a book club provides common ground for satisfying conversations about questions, ideas, and situations raised in the book. To that end, you may want to give copies to family members simultaneously.

Posts on social media are greatly appreciated, especially those that include a picture of you and the book. Please tag the author: @JanisseRay and @tracklesswild.

Possible hashtags include: #woodsoffannincounty #janisseray #newfiction #debutnovel #bookrelease #southernfiction #read #amreading #story #newread #bookclub #bookinmyhand

Unlike most books, this novel does not include endorsements from other writers, and instead it relies on the opinions of readers like you. Reviews on Goodreads, Amazon, and other book sites—as well as reviews in blogs, online journals, newsletters, and print media— are most welcome.

To arrange an interview, speaking engagement, workshop, or virtual visit, please contact the author via her website, www.janisseray.com.

Your support of books, reading, and writers makes a story like this possible. Thank you.

BIOGRAPHY

Janisse Ray is an American writer who explores the borderland of nature and culture. This is her first novel. Ray has won an American Book Award, Pushcart Prize, Southern Bookseller Award, Southern Environmental Law Center Writing Award, Nautilus Award, and Eisenberg Award, among many others. Her bestselling first book, ECOLOGY OF A CRACKER CHILDHOOD, was a NEW YORK TIMES Notable. Her latest collection of essays, WILD SPECTACLE, won the Donald L. Jordan Prize for Literary Excellence, which carries a $10,000 prize. Ray serves on the editorial board of terrain.org and is an honorary member of the Association for the Study of Literature and the Environment. She earned an MFA from the University of Montana, has received two honorary doctorates, and has been inducted into the Georgia Writers Hall of Fame. Ray lives and works inland from Savannah, Georgia.

Website | **www.janisseray.com**
Facebook Author Page | **www.facebook.com/ReadJanisseRay**
Instagram | **@tracklesswild**
Twitter | **@tracklesswild**
Email | **janisse.ray1@gmail.com**
Substack | **tracklesswild.substack.com**

Made in the USA
Las Vegas, NV
20 September 2022

55511051R00115